SHATTERED

SHATTERED
By Valerie Davisson
Copyright © 2019 Valerie Davisson

SHATTERED is a work of fiction. Names, characters, places, and incidents are the product of the author's imagination or are used fictitiously. Any resemblance to actual events, locales, businesses, or persons, living or dead, is coincidental.

Published by Vaughn House Publishing, Depoe Bay, OR
Second Edition
Previously Published by Hauser Publishing in 2014
Print ISBN - 978-0-9838696-1-0
Ebook ISBN - 978-0-9838696-3-4

Cover and Interior Design by Kimberly Peticolas, www.kimpeticolas.com

Library of Congress Control Number: 2019910307

10   9   8   7   6   5   4   3   2   1

SHATTERED

A Logan McKenna Novel

VALERIE DAVISSON

*To my sister, Michelle, whose strength and loyalty
provided the inspiration for Logan. Love you, Sis!*

PROLOGUE

The last time she'd seen a dead body, it was Jack's. And it had lain neatly resting in a long, cool coffin, peaceful, far removed from the sights and sounds of death.

Not this one.

Someone had angrily stuffed this one into a white cinder block box—a space much too small for it, like a bundle of human garbage. Neck broken, legs bent like a spider's, jeans drenched in blood, and an almost unrecognizable, bloated, purple-veined face. But she did recognize it, and it belonged to someone much too young to die.

1

AN EVENING EARLY IN MAY

Traces of smoke from distant beach bonfires, mingled with the juxtaposed scents of eucalyptus and jasmine, filled the night. A woodsy aroma rose from the fresh layer of bark chips the groundskeepers had put down earlier in the day. If Southern California had a signature scent, this was it.

Seated on a stool at his workbench in the back, Thomas contemplated his next move. The storage unit he worked in was just an old tent from which they kept the front booth stocked. Canvas walls stretched back about ten feet, supported by a crisscross network of sturdy metal poles. A side flap opened to a warm canyon breeze.

On the rough surface in front of him lay a thin piece of obsidian, measuring a little more than six inches long. It had been carefully knapped, sloping down to a fine edge on either side. The resulting ultra-sharp blade could easily slice through the bones of the hands that made it. Four completed knives lay to his right. A battery-powered work lamp illuminated the area directly in front of him on the table, providing enough light by which to work.

On a narrow shelf just above the obsidian blade lay several curved pieces of antlers ready to be made into knife handles. Elk, not deer. Customers probably wouldn't know the difference if he used deer antler, but he would. The German collector, on the other hand, knew his stuff. He'd insisted on elk.

Thomas considered each piece.

Just as he started to reach for one, his cell phone rang. Placing his materials down on the table, he wiped his hands on his jeans, reached in his pocket, pulled out the phone and answered.

"Hello . . . everything okay?"

Thomas lowered his voice, even though no one else was around.

"Did you get the money?" he asked. "Good."

"Are you sure you can handle this?" he added. "Okay. I just want this to be over."

Thomas ended the call and slid the phone back in his pocket. Satisfied there was nothing more he could do for now, he refocused on his work. Looking over the antler pieces one more time, he reached up and selected one, hefted it briefly and placed it on the table. Holding the long, obsidian blade carefully in the other hand, he held it against one end and then the other of the future handle, trying to decide which angle worked best.

He loved working at night. No interruptions or customers asking questions. The quiet was deep but something made him stop, sit up, and listen. Pinpricks ran up his spine. He rubbed the back of his neck and shook it off. Probably nothing.

Still.

Turning slowly, he looked over his left shoulder. He was not alone.

One of the young glassblowers, Elizabeth, leaned coolly against the metal post in the doorway formed by the open flap, arms folded. Not a hair out of place, her thin ponytail cut a perfect, white-blond scythe out of the soft, night sky. Oozing confidence, her face looked deceptively delicate in the residual light from the lamp. It also looked smug.

You only had to meet Elizabeth once to know she was trouble. Keeping a tight lid on his mouth and his emotions, Thomas wondered how much she had heard.

"Sounds very hush, hush, Thomas. Keeping secrets from the wife? Gambling? Get someone pregnant?" Elizabeth fished, her blue eyes glittering like tiny chunks of Arctic ice.

Thomas decided to wait her out.

When he neither denied nor confirmed, she continued, strolling into the tent, "What's the money for? Let me guess . . . an abortion? Something worse?"

Thomas crossed his arms and leaned back on the counter, quickly calculating the damage and what he could do about it, careful not to let his face betray his mounting concern. Whichever way this went down, he would protect Lisa. Of that one thing, he was very sure.

Elizabeth paused, looked down at her feet, and straightened her shoulders. With something bordering on an apology she looked directly into his eyes.

"This isn't personal, Thomas. I didn't plan to overhear your conversation tonight. But I've learned to take luck where I find it.

"So, I don't know who you paid to do what, but as long as you're writing checks, you can send some my way. $8,000 ought to do it."

She waited to see if this amount would fly. Thomas didn't object, so she continued.

"I need airfare for the competition, and I'm short some to set up my own studio. When I get back, whether I win or not, I'm going solo. I'm tired of dealing with troglodytes like Matt."

She almost spit out the name. Elizabeth squinted at him, waiting to determine the efficacy of her threat.

Thomas wasn't sure what she was capable of, but she looked dead serious. He'd only met her once before, when he was out visiting Howard at his compound where he and his interns lived and Howard gave classes. She'd half-heartedly hit on him. He'd politely, but firmly, made it clear he was married and that had been the end of it. In fact, he thought she was seeing Matt, one of the other glassblowers, but after what she'd just said, that didn't seem likely. He hoped she wasn't the type to hold a grudge.

Apparently that had nothing to do with it, because she didn't act like a woman scorned, just one on a mission, and after overhearing his conversation, an opportunity to fulfill it— with his money.

Thomas had about $20,000 in the bank. He'd just gotten a large order from his German collector. That's why he was working so hard now, he had to replace his inventory before the festival. Luckily, Elizabeth didn't know this or she'd have asked for more.

$10,000 was already going to the man on the phone, so $8,000 was doable. Adopting Elizabeth's pragmatic attitude, he went to the bank in the morning and withdrew that amount. It was from his business account, which Lisa never checked. Until recently, it wouldn't have been worth it if she did, as the balance rarely rose above $150. If she ever discovered the missing money, he would just have to explain what it was for.

Money meant nothing. He'd do anything to protect his wife.

2

FRIDAY, MAY 31

Logan tossed the letter back on her desk. She'd definitely landed in the City of Oz and was in dire need of a pair of ruby slippers.

Not for the first time this year, she wondered why anyone would work in the public school system unless they had a lobotomy or were working off jail time. It all started last October when, as a favor to her friend Bonnie, she'd taken a long-term sub job for a seventh grade teacher at Roosevelt Middle School in Tilcott, CA.

She'd spent the last two years since her husband Jack died wrapping up and selling the computer business they'd built together. The process had been wrenching. After paying off business debts—Jack had been more charmer than money manager—there wasn't a whole lot left.

Truth be told, she needed the job.

Tilcott was a small community, about twenty minutes up the coast from the even smaller town of Jasper, where she and

Bonnie had grown up. Top scores on the entry exam and a double major in Math and Music qualified her for an Emergency Teaching Credential. If she decided to continue, she'd have to enter the internship program next year. They had one that started in June, completing her coursework in the summer.

She quickly discovered that things had changed since she, or even her daughter Amy, had been in school. The focus on test scores had left students burned out, teachers exhausted, and parents frustrated. Music and art programs had been eliminated in order to hire test prep coaches. They would have eliminated PE, too, but a few enlightened state legislators had managed to mandate a minimum of forty minutes a week. Of course, few districts enforced this requirement.

Any subject not specifically tested was given short shrift, so science and history were pretty much ignored in favor of hours of back-to-basics reading and math lessons, keeping students chained to their desks for hours. Who did they think was going to make the new discoveries for clean energy and find the cure for cancer? Someone who'd never done a science experiment?

Lucky for her students, Logan chose to ignore all that nonsense. She took her students out for PE every day. Her first-day-of-school speech went something like this:

"Here's the deal. I don't give stickers for breathing. I will never lie to you. I can help you learn to write anything from a business plan to a Dear John letter, but I won't write it for you. In five short years, you'll be running this planet, so I expect you to know something about it before June.

"I'll give you the tools and the skills, you'll give yourselves the world. First assignment of the year? Teach me something tomorrow that I don't know. Any questions?"

SHATTERED

Thirty-six pairs of wide eyes stared back at her. No alphabet necklace in sight, and none of her jewelry lit up. She was definitely different, but could she be trusted?

By the end of the first month, everyone knew the tall, new teacher with the long, wavy hair said what she meant and meant what she said. Sun glinting off her auburn locks, her trademark boot-and-jeans stride was easily spotted from across campus, usually accompanied by one or more students.

By January, when her down-to-earth teaching style started producing results, requests to be in her class started piling up in the office. Not only were her students among the few with smiles on their faces Monday morning and books under their arms on Friday afternoons, but most of them outperformed other students on the mid-year math and reading tests.

That was the beginning of the trouble.

Sheila Morell, an eighth grade teacher at the school and one of Principal Metterson's favorites, said nothing but rolled her eyes and sighed audibly in the staff meeting when the results were announced.

Not satisfied with gossip and innuendo, Sheila had gone to Metterson and convinced him to write this pack-of-lies letter on Logan's desk, accusing her of helping her students cheat on the tests in order to 'win.'

"Win what?!" Logan had vented to Bonnie on the phone at break that morning.

"What exactly do I win? What is wrong with that woman?"

"Too much to mention," Bonnie said.

"And I'd actually considered taking this damn job!" Logan fumed. She wasn't sure she'd take it now if they handed it to her on a silver platter.

"Fly low, okay?" Bonnie said, "You have until August, right? You don't have to make any decisions until then."

"Yeah, I guess."

"Just because they're accusing you doesn't mean the board will believe them."

But hope was dim at best. She knew no one on the school board and had done nothing to ingratiate herself with anyone at district. Why should they fight for her? She was well aware that all five feet eight inches of her was really lousy at office politics. Working for herself, she just hadn't had to deal with it in a long time.

Stuffing the letter into her purse, she focused on the task at hand. Clear green eyes scanned the end-of-the-year checklist given to everyone by the school secretary.

Computers covered and stored? Check.

Bulletin boards stripped? Check.

Textbook inventory complete? Check . . . Check . . . Check!

Lesson plans made for the first week back?

"If there's going to be a first week back," she muttered.

Later she would process the year, but right now the only thing she wanted to process was an ice-cold margarita at Juan's. If she left now, she might beat traffic and fit in a beach run before dinner.

"Look on the bright side," Logan told herself as she locked her door for the summer, and maybe for good. "You have seventy-six white squares on your calendar; you're a free woman until September!"

She was looking forward to a relaxing, uneventful summer.

3

L ola awaited.

Still a looker at fifty-five, and in amazing shape, Lola was Logan's '58 Corvette. Of course, being a Californian, she'd had a little work done, but her chassis was original. The gleaming classic sports car had been her father's surprise gift for her when she graduated from the University of California Irvine (UCI). She remembered the day she'd first seen one, parked outside a movie theater, looking low and sexy, and unlike any car she'd seen before. Her favorite part was the 'scoops.' It looked like a huge lion had swiped a chunk out of each side from the front wheel to about mid-door, leaving impressive, chrome claw marks behind.

Chrome-heavy, the original '58 Corvette didn't handle all that well, but after her mechanic magician, Mr. Delgado, finished tweaking everything, adding power and subtracting weight, Lola not only hugged the curves, but flew past seventy without a shimmy.

Exhaling the breath she hadn't realized she'd been holding, Logan grinned widely, lowered the cloth top, threw her purse onto the passenger-side floorboard and tucked herself neatly into the lovingly restored, creamy white leather interior. She fired her up, waved again to Cindy, the school secretary, who smiled at her through the office window, and headed for the Pacific Coast Highway (PCH) and home.

Home! Just the sound of that word made her smile. Being a homeowner was a luxury she still wasn't used to. The purchase of the house took the last of her reserves from the sale of the business, but it had been worth it.

Eyes half closed, she let the powerful purr of Lola's V-8 and the bracing ocean air push all other thoughts from her mind. Traffic had already backed up on the SR-55 and the I-405, but PCH was still clear when she turned onto it off of MacArthur, heading south to Jasper and her new home. This is why she lived in Southern California. Twenty minutes later she was idling at the first of seven stoplights in her small hometown.

Being near the beach was half the reason Logan had chosen her property from among the three or four in her price range the Realtor had assured her were 'just perfect.' One property was located on Killer Hill. Aptly named by the locals, Killer Hill had ruined more than one transmission and kept most tourists to Oak Street, looking for an easier route to the restaurants and definitely an easier place to park. Logan loved it.

Lacking a utility room, adequate guest parking, and twentieth-century plumbing, the property had not been the pick of the litter. Gamely clinging to Killer's breast, it was originally the caretaker's cottage of a larger estate; but time and squabbling inheritors had cut it off from the main house, which was now the public library, a few streets away.

The saving graces of the small, two-story home were its solid construction, tall French doors, and a flat rooftop with a view of the ocean. She could already feel the joy of playing her violin, Bella up there, looking out over the water as the sun went down.

SHATTERED

One walkthrough and Logan bargained half-heartedly and signed quickly. Cash on the barrel, in less than twenty-four hours the house was hers. It had been sitting vacant for six months since the owner, local writer Meg Carlton, died, and the relatives, who lived in Indiana, were only too happy to sell it without first fixing it up.

When the light changed, Logan drove by the "Welcome to Jasper" sign at the intersection of Ocean and PCH. To the right lay a small grassy park and an old, wooden boardwalk bordered by a soft, sandy beach dotted with volleyball nets. The tide was coming in and a couple of kids were skim boarding.

The next stoplight was her street. She shifted into first and turned left. A coffee house called Tava'e's anchored the corner on the right. Sounded Samoan or Tongan, maybe? She never could keep them straight. Polynesian, anyway. When the light turned green, she made the sharp turn and shifted into second. Lola took the corner well, making it through a yellow—as she was wont to do—and began pulling up Killer Hill.

4

The next morning, after a quick wakeup shower, Logan stepped into her last pair of clean shorts, a sports bra, and a tank top. She'd have to get to a laundromat soon, and a grocery store for supplies.

Energized by the bright sun streaming in her window and the thought of a golden summer stretching out before her, a welcome shiver of anticipation launched Logan into action. Feeling better than she had in months, she practically skipped down the stairs like a twelve-year-old about to ride her new bike, grabbed her tennis shoes and, balancing on one foot, was tying the second shoe when someone knocked on the door.

Just before 8:00 a.m. on a Saturday. She wasn't expecting anyone. She finished tying a quick double knot and opened the door.

"Good Morning!"

A Viking stood in her doorway. A tousle-headed, blonde Viking with muddy tennis shoes, open blue eyes, and two cups of steaming coffee, one in each hand. He was losing the battle to maintain control of the two cups plus a greasy paper bag. A couple of napkins drifted to the floor. The smell of cinnamon was captivating.

Amused and salivating, Logan invited him in. He introduced himself as he was wiping his feet.

"Hi, I'm your neighbor, Ben. Saw your upstairs bathroom window was steamed up, so figured you were up . . . Oh!" the Viking stumbled momentarily, ". . . don't worry, I can't see you . . . your . . .you're up higher than I am . . . ."

She wished she could think of something to save him, but he just powered on, completely red in the face.

"Thought you might not have everything set up yet and could use some coffee." He stuck out his hand and offered her one of the hot paper cups. "Of course, you might not even drink coffee . . . I could have gotten you tea . . . I . . ."

"No, this is great, thanks. Nice to meet you, Ben. I've seen you working in your yard," she said, accepting the to-go cup gingerly, gesturing toward his property with it. "Your yard looks great, by the way. Looks like a professional did it."

He hadn't looked so tall grubbing around the junipers.

She quickly switched her grip to the top and bottom edges of the cup to prevent burning her fingers.

"Figured you might not have unpacked your coffeemaker yet," he said.

"Well, if I had a coffeemaker, you're right, it wouldn't be unpacked yet," she said.

Ben looked at the empty living room. She didn't elaborate and he didn't ask.

"Which means I can't offer you a place to sit . . ." she said.

The only furniture she had was a loaner bed from Bonnie and a three-legged stool. She hadn't had time to go shopping, but now that school was out, she had no excuse. It was on her to do list.

"That's okay," Ben said, "I just stopped by to say hello and welcome you to the neighborhood. My nephews are coming over and I need to walk Purgatory before they get here, anyway. Purgatory's my dog, you'll have to meet him —and my nephews, sometime."

"I look forward to being formally introduced to Purgatory," Logan said with mock seriousness, "as well as your nephews."

Was she flirting? He really was an attractive man.

Ben promised to bring them over once she got settled, and the dog, sooner than that. They talked for another few minutes, then he handed her the paper bag on his way out.

"Breakfast of champions," he promised.

Breakfast turned out to be one of the largest and best tasting cinnamon rolls Logan had ever had. As she sank her teeth into the gooey, tender goodness, she watched Ben walk back to his place. Licking vanilla frosting off her lips, Logan realized how much she had missed male conversation this last year.

In their computer business, she and Jack worked with both men and women, but her coworkers at the middle school were almost all female—Metterson not matching her definition of a man—or a human being for that matter. Just thinking about him and that hateful letter made her blood boil. She pushed all thoughts of her work problems to the back of her mind and brought thoughts of Ben to the foreground.

She liked him, but knew this might be trouble. Ben was a neighbor.

"I need friends right now, not a lover!" she told herself firmly, picking up Dimebox, her tortoiseshell rescue cat, as he wandered by, nuzzling her nose in his neck as he tried to wriggle away.

She had celebrated her first month of home ownership by going down to the pound and adopting the scrawny ball of fur. Underfed and feasted on by fleas, the tiny kitten had been almost too tired to rub against the finger she'd offered him through the wire on his cage. It was love at first sight.

She'd scooped him up, cleaned him up and named him after her grandfather's birthplace, the tiny West-Texas town of Dimebox, thus named because it was no bigger than a dime box of snuff. As she filled out the paperwork and wrote the check, Dimebox snuggled trustingly in the crook of her left elbow.

Within six weeks of Science Diet and love, the weak kitten would pack on fourteen pounds and become the terror of the neighborhood—but Logan didn't know that, so bought him a tiny collar he would outgrow in a week.

Logan gave him a squeeze before putting him back down.

"Onward and upward!" she announced, going into the kitchen to throw away her trash.

She had a lot to do this weekend if she was going to be ready to help Thomas and Lisa at their booth at the Otter Festival on Monday.

5

There was a white wall where a dresser should have been. Logan blinked her eyes to focus as thousands of neurons fired to make sense of this information.

No dirty socks on the floor. No jacket hanging on the hook by the closet. No delicious smell of coffee rose to greet her, and when she reached her hand across the sheets for the thousandth time, the other side of the bed was not warm.

Jack wasn't at a rugby game. And he wasn't coming home. For a moment pain flooded in with the sunshine, unexpectedly sharp. She wondered if there would come a time when these sneak attacks of grief would fade, or if she would want them to. Survivor's guilt required she endure them.

The shrill alarm jolted her fully awake. Reaching out blindly, trying to hit the snooze button and missing several times, she finally succeeded in killing the keening beast by yanking the cord out of the wall. When she could afford it, she promised herself to get one of those alarms that gradually wake you with gentle sounds of chirping birds, babbling streams, or Yo-Yo Ma.

Grateful for a reason to pull herself out of impending depression, Logan rolled sideways out of bed, touching her toes down lightly on the hardwood floor, enjoying the feel of it under her feet.

One step at a time.

Thinking of the coffee she would have to go out for because she had no coffeemaker yet, Logan sloughed off her pajamas and padded sleepily toward the shower. She doubted the Viking delivered on Mondays. He was probably at work by now. She turned the nozzle on as hot as she could stand it and, for the next ten minutes, let it pound on her shoulders, easing tight muscles.

In her old life, in addition to making the coffee on the days he had early morning rugby practice, Jack had always turned on the shower so it'd be warm when she got in. It was just one of the small pleasures of married life she had to get used to living without.

"As if that were the major one," she mumbled.

Fully awake now, turning up the water pressure, Logan blasted her libido into submission.

Today.

Focus on today.

Otter Festival.

Every summer in her teen years, as far back as she could remember, Logan worked at Jasper's most popular, annual summer event, dubbed the "Otter Arts Festival" because of the large numbers of the friendly beasts that used to populate the giant kelp beds off shore.

Even though they were hunted to near extinction years ago due to their beautiful pelts and playful natures, they remained part of the local culture and identity. Every shop in town had at least one t-shirt, key-chain, or sculpture of otters floating on their backs, cracking open shells on their stomachs to get to the sweet meat inside. Though several previous attempts to coax remaining otter populations in the Bay Area to expand south had failed, residents remained ever optimistic they'd return someday.

Water running lukewarm, Logan quickly rinsed her hair and got out, briskly drying off with one of the thick, soft towels Bonnie had given her for a housewarming gift. Deciding against the whole spend-an-hour-to-blow-dry–and-smooth-it routine, Logan opted for the natural look, which involved nothing more than a leave-in conditioner. She gave her hair a final, cursory finger comb and pronounced it acceptable. Peach lip-gloss, a swipe of bronzer and a quick glance in the bathroom mirror and she was good to go.

With a natural athlete's unconscious grace, Logan strode barefoot across the room. In one movement, she scooped up Dimebox and kissed the top of his head, then released him and went to find something to wear.

Men had always found Logan attractive, but Jack gave her the most original compliment of all, calling her a sexier version of Katherine Hepburn. "All woman, with just enough testosterone to kick my butt!"

She possessed the same independent, hard-working streak for which the actress was famous. Both had been lucky enough to find men they loved, but not the luck to keep them. Katherine, by way of Spencer Tracy being married, and Logan by the car accident that took Jack's life.

She wondered if, like Hepburn, she was now destined to spend the rest of her life alone. It turned out all right for Hepburn, if interviews with the famous actress were accurate.

Learn to love the things you cannot change.

Yep, it was all about attitude.

One plain white cotton t-shirt and jeans later, all of Logan's major fashion decisions were made for the day. Boots completed the look. One black pair, one brown—she had shoes for every occasion.

Downstairs, after making sure the kitchen window was open a crack, she swirled some fresh water into the cat's water dish, grabbed her keys, locked the front door, heading out for the festival and the first real day of summer.

6

Part of Logan wanted to spend the whole summer hibernating, putzing around in her slippers, nesting, or fiddling when she felt like it, but she knew too much time alone wasn't what she needed right now.

"Depression can be an oh-so-tempting blanket in which to wrap oneself," a grief counselor had warned.

So, when her old friend, Thomas Delgado and his wife, Lisa, asked her to help them out in their booth at the festival, she said yes. She was going to be playing a few nights down there anyway to pick up a little extra cash, so she'd been happy to oblige. Only recently had she started playing her fiddle again.

Just enough June gloom to keep it cool until early afternoon, it was a gorgeous Southern California morning. Grabbing a scrunchie from the glove compartment, checking her reflection in the rearview mirror, she managed to pull most of her thick waves up into a ponytail. Near enough.

It was definitely a top-down day. Unless it was pouring rain, every day was a top-down day as far as Logan was concerned. Checking over her shoulder, she backed out onto the street, selected her cruising soundtrack. Edith Piaf's distinctive growl flew out of the speakers, washing over her.

About twenty minutes later, "*Je ne regrette rien . . . ,*" the fifth song on the CD, was winding down as Lola's tires crunched into the employee parking lot. The maintenance crew laid down a fresh layer of gravel in anticipation of the heavy summer tourist parking. Other than that, it hadn't changed much in the twenty-odd years since she'd been there, her last summer before graduation.

Traffic was light, so she arrived in plenty of time, parked, and walked toward the vendor entrance in the back. Thomas told her their booth wouldn't be hard to find, they were just beyond the new glassblowers' area, a great location.

A familiar voice rooted Logan to the spot.

"Well, I'll be damned," Logan said to herself, shaking her head in disbelief when she saw who was manning the entrance. With a big smile, she got in line to check in.

Iona Slatterly.

Everybody had to check in. Iona saw to that. Listening to Iona bark instructions, Logan felt transported back to high school. Stuffed into pink jeans, the petite woman perched on a tall stool next to a plastic, folding table covered with parking stickers and badges, managing a growing line. "Sticker . . . Badge . . . Sticker . . . Badge."

Iona looked up. "Logan McKenna! Welcome back. Sorry to hear about Jack. It couldn't have been easy, losing him so soon after we lost your dad. I miss your dad. He was a good man."

Logan noticed she didn't say the same about Jack. Unfazed by Iona's directness, Logan said thanks, took the items handed to her and signed in. Iona had been a fixture at the festival as far back as anyone could remember.

Where did one find pink jeans anyway? The girls' department at Sears? A long-sleeve, white blouse with western piping was neatly tucked into the jeans and cinched with a white, rhinestone-studded belt. The woman couldn't weigh as much as some of her seventh graders. Platinum-blonde hair, ratted into an immobile French twist with two perfect ringlets on each side, was sprayed to withstand any and all of Iona's activities; which, as rumor had it, were prodigious.

A solid roll of bangs sat atop starkly penciled brows. Today's lipstick was Neon Geranium. With a No. 2 pencil tucked behind her ear, Iona was concentrating on the vendor list attached to the clipboard in front of her. A Marlboro Light burned on the edge of a can of Pepsi near her left hand.

After Logan accepted her badge and parking sticker, she returned to the parking lot to hang the latter on her car's mirror, then pinned on her identification badge and docilely reentered the festival grounds under Iona's watchful eye and ongoing instructions.

"Employee entrance closes at 9:00 a.m. sharp! After that you have to use the front gate, and you'll be charged admission without your badge! We lock up tighter than a drum at 11:00 p.m., people. Don't forget, or you'll find yourself spending the night curled up in your booth . . . It's happened before! . . . Look alive there, Sonny . . . here, let me do that . . . ."

Logan could still hear Iona for a good twenty yards more as she passed the food vendors. The food court had the typical offerings: Chinese, Greek, hamburgers, and hot dogs. People may get tired of egg rolls or Greek salad, but no one ever got tired of Phoenix burgers. Logan's mouth watered as the smell of grilled onions and thick meat patties drifted toward her. She promised herself she'd circle back for provisions after she found Thomas' booth.

Nothing about the fair was linear, so after a couple of twists and turns on the hilly path, in the middle of a clearing, surrounded by four or five artists' booths, sat one of the newest, and certainly one of the most popular additions to the Otter

Arts Festival, the impressive glassblowers' cage. No one was working in the cage yet, but two people were setting up inside.

"There! Not *there*, you idiot!" yelled a man at a worker wearing canvas gloves, hauling a large, heavy bag of what looked like sand.

A thick, wheat-colored braid hung straight down the worker's back, and it took a minute for Logan to realize it was a young woman. Logan was surprised she let the man talk to her that way, but it wasn't her battle. The girl would have to learn to stick up for herself.

As she wandered through the fair, Logan noticed the festival was definitely getting upscale. She remembered more candles-and-incense booths than master woodworkers, jewelers and glassblowers when she'd worked there in her teens. Even so, some familiar faces greeted her as she walked by. After stopping to catch up with a few old friends, she found Thomas and Lisa's booth.

7

"Hey, Cochise!" Logan called.

"Hey, White Girl!"

Thomas hadn't changed a bit. Unfolding himself, he came down off the ladder propped against the back wall of the booth. Worn jeans hung easily on his lean body, topped by a t-shirt of indeterminate color. The only new clothing item, a pair of red, Converse tennis shoes.

Thomas looked pretty much the same as he did in high school. When he smiled, all white teeth and chiseled cheekbones, shiny, black-as-coal, chin-length hair tucked behind his ears and onyx eyes, he looked every inch the movie star Indian.

Lisa did not.

Five-four to her husband's five-eleven, from the back Lisa was true to her Crow lineage: a short, stocky figure and stick-straight black hair that came down to her shoulder blades. Until she turned around.

This produced a startling effect on most people. Two lavender-blue eyes, fringed with long, black lashes were set in a delicate, ivory face, sprinkled with freckles. This side of her genetics came from a porcelain-skinned blonde archaeologist named Barbara who came to the reservation to round out her PhD, but fell in love with Lisa's grandfather and rounded out her belly instead.

Lisa was the only Indian Logan knew who needed sunscreen.

Thomas enveloped Logan in a hug, "Good to see you, how's Lola?"

Thomas Delgado's father was the miracle-working mechanic who kept Lola in shape. No one could pronounce his Lakota name, so everyone just called him Mr. Delgado. His mother was descended from California ranchero royalty, so he took her name.

Logan wouldn't think of entrusting Lola to anyone else. Mr. Delgado was the best. People with classic cars drove up from San Diego and down from LA for his expertise. Jay Leno even brought him up to his place once to administer to an ailing '56 Chevy of his. Like his son, Delgado was quiet—never said two words when one would do—but he knew his stuff.

"Great. Tell your dad I said hi. If he didn't do such a good job with Lola, I'd see him more often."

In a quieter voice Thomas asked, "How are you doing?"

"Good, I'm doing okay. Where's Lisa?"

Brushing sawdust off her pants, Lisa got up from filling display cases, came around the corner, and gave Logan a huge hug. After the usual hellos, she took her behind the counter where they could sit down on stools and she could show her the new pieces.

Logan admired the new bead and quillwork Lisa had completed over the winter, including a beautiful cradle cap, and Thomas' impressive display of obsidian knives with bone handles. Thomas had recently left academia to work full time recreating the beautiful artifacts people rarely got to see because they were locked up in museums.

"Are you sure you want to spend your summer hustling trade beads?" Lisa said.

She took a drink from her water bottle, but looked up again, with some concern in her eyes.

"Thomas's cousin, Jerry, is coming down from Coeur d'Alene, so if you need more time . . . if you just want to relax this summer . . . "

"No, I'm good", Logan reassured her. "I'm looking forward to this. It's great seeing everyone—I mean, a lot of things have changed, but it's the same festival.

"Are you going to play?" asked Lisa.

"Yes!" Logan's face brightened. "I'm sitting in with Ned for Sal. I promised I'd fill in for her after the baby."

Logan wondered how long it would be before people stopped thinking of her as Logan, the woman whose husband died two years ago, and just plain Logan, the person. Her husband had died; she hadn't. She wanted to regain herself, or at least find out who she was without Jack. And playing Bella again was a significant first step.

Thomas climbed the ladder again, not satisfied with the angle of the bow he'd just hung, and Logan started helping Lisa flatten boxes. They worked easily for the next hour.

Lisa asked, "How do you like teaching?"

"The kids are great. Teaching is the easy part; it's the bulletin-board wars I don't get." Logan flattened some boxes Lisa had just emptied, with a little more force than necessary, while Lisa looked for a place on the counter to put the cash register.

"I wouldn't have the patience for it," Lisa said.

"Yeah. I really like the kids, but if it wasn't for Bonnie, I think I'd have given up by Christmas."

Logan stomped the next box into total submission. She wasn't ready to talk about the letter yet. No sense burdening her friends. Thomas glanced down, raised an eyebrow, and Lisa laughed.

"I can always teach you how to bead," Lisa offered innocently.

They both knew Logan's questionable skill with a needle. The one summer Lisa had tried to teach her, Logan had mangled a perfectly good dream catcher so badly, Thomas declared it unfit to catch anything but nightmares in some New Ager's bedroom.

Thomas and Lisa traveled the powwow circuit as much as they could, including the big mid-June one in San Bernardino, about an hour and a half inland from Jasper. They'd invited Logan to come with them and experience one first-hand. Lisa was dancing in several events and was working on a dress she'd embellished for one of the other dancers.

A couple of hours later, when they'd finished unpacking and tagged enough arrowheads, knives, bead and quill work to fill the cases, Lisa stood up and announced, "Okay, I think that's enough. We've earned some lunch."

"Double cheese with Fire Fries for me," called Thomas from the truck, where he was stacking the empty boxes. "And a Coke."

"Okay!" Lisa said. Already half out the booth, she pulled her purse from under the counter and looked to Logan for her order.

"I'll come with. Are meals included in my compensation package? If so, you're going to lose money—" she said.

"Oh, and pick up a couple of churros, too" came the disembodied voice from the truck.

"That's how Thomas keeps his girlish figure," said Lisa, rolling her eyes.

8

The Otter Arts Festival sprawled over two hillside acres between PCH and the low, coastal mountains to the west. Originally little more than a scattering of tents and other temporary buildings, over the years, as more artists moved to Jasper and people started driving down from Santa Barbara or up from San Diego to escape the crowds, they formed a cooperative and raised money for more permanent digs.

Public restrooms replaced Porta-Potties, and a stunning oceanic sculpture, created by the famous Solange Sauvage, also the owner of the festival, now graced the main entrance.

Artists' booths scattered themselves along a twisting warren of hilly paths. The only open space was in the center of the festival, about twenty feet from a hill that rose steeply behind it.

Glassblowing demonstrations and surrounding booths filled with the glassblowers' wares drew the crowds that in large part kept the festival solvent. Prime real estate for vendors was anywhere near the glassblowing cage.

Logan and Lisa continued toward the food court, but didn't get far.

"Lisa!"

A tall woman with steel-wool hair enveloped Lisa in a massive, maternal hug.

"Rose! You're squishing me!" Lisa objected, laughing.

Teetering towers of boxes and a beautiful maple spinning wheel fronted a small but neat booth. Rose was still getting set up.

"What new stuff did you make this year? I pray for rain so I can wear my lamb's wool scarf."

After promising to get together soon, Rose went back into her booth to finish unpacking, leaving Logan and Lisa to continue down the path.

Coming up on their left was the gaudy, gingerbread booth belonging to Neva Schultz. Both women knew Neva from way back. She was one of the original artists, if you could call her that, and many didn't, from the early days of the festival. Pushing seventy now, Neva sold gaudy Christmas ornaments, potholders, and toaster warmers with 'Jasper' embroidered on them and other kitsch that, surprisingly, sold well enough to keep her spot year after year.

"Something for everyone," Lisa muttered, as they approached.

"Whatever happened to her little boy?" Logan asked.

"Danny? Last time I saw him he wasn't very little anymore. He must be in his late teens, early twenties by now? Big kid."

"Do you think he moved out on his own? He was kind of high-functioning, wasn't he?"

"Yeah. Hope so, for his sake. He was always a sweet kid."

Logan looked in the booth as they passed and was startled to see Neva crouched inside, half-hidden in shadow. She didn't know if Neva had heard Lisa's comments or was glaring because that was her permanent expression.

Involuntarily, Logan shuddered.

SHATTERED

Neva immediately got up and stood in the doorway, turning her back to them, blocking their view of the interior.

Okay then. That was weird. It's not like they were going to steal any of her artistic ideas.

Neva's was the last booth in the semicircle. The path then ended directly at a growing line in front of Phoenix Burgers. After ordering three of everything, Logan grabbed salt, extra sauce, straws and napkins. Loaded up, the two women retraced their steps.

Thomas cleared a space for the three of them and pulled out folding stools from the storage tent. For the next twenty minutes, they ate in contented silence. At one point during their meal, Thomas reached over and gently wiped a drip of sauce from the corner of Lisa's mouth. Logan felt an unexpected stab of loneliness.

She was glad she'd said yes to helping Thomas and Lisa out in this year's festival, and to playing her beloved violin, Bella, again. Two whole months far away from the mess at school. Two months of making some money to restore her depleted bank account. Two months working with her good friends.

This summer was exactly what she needed.

9

All the shoppers at the festival reminded Logan she wanted to pick up a thank you gift for Bonnie. She and Mike had done so much for her after the accident.

Bonnie had three sets of china, matching throw pillows on the couch, and all of her houseplants were alive, so something for her house seemed appropriate. Maybe something from one of the glassblowers. The festival had only been open a couple of days and Logan still hadn't made it over there. She wanted to watch a demonstration anyway, so took a long lunch break and headed over just as two men entered the cage.

It really was a cage. Along the bottom of the structure ran a rock wall about three feet high. Rising up from the wall was strong metal fencing, like mega chicken wire, ostensibly protecting onlookers, allowing the glassblowers to be observed on all four sides as they demonstrated their ancient art and showed off for the crowds. At ten by twenty-four feet, there was enough room for two glassblowers to work in tandem, although Lisa said some artists worked alone. Demo about to start, Logan settled in to watch.

The taller glassblower, a nice-looking man in his twenties, reminded Logan of Amy's first boyfriend. He wore his sandy hair a little long over the ears and had an open, amiable expression on his face. He looked like one of those people whose parts were equal to their sum. No mysterious layers, no guile, just a nice kid in old, soft jeans, sandals, and a t-shirt. Whatever logo it had at one time couldn't be read now.

The second glassblower Logan recognized right away as the jerk she had seen barking orders at the young woman yesterday. Intense looking, young but not youthful, probably born with that scowl. Squat and muscular, he had almost blue-white skin and stiff, black hair. Although it was only noon, he sported a five o'clock shadow. Thick, curly chest hair sprouted out of the top of his t-shirt.

His right wrist was wrapped with what looked like a frayed Ace bandage. The overall impression was of a meaty gladiator, slightly round-shouldered, standing his ground against the world. She imagined him at dinner, one arm wrapped protectively around his plate, the other shoveling food into his mouth. Although shorter than the other man, this one took command of the large space easily—obviously the one in charge.

While the taller one moved at an easy pace about the cage, checking gauges and equipment in the background, pouring some colored glass chips on a steel table, the other man addressed the gathering audience. The same young woman she saw before set a gallon jug of ice water on a metal stand inside the door.

"Thanks Leah," the tall man said, lifting his chin in greeting, since his hands were full. She favored him with a dazzling smile. Must be her boyfriend, Logan thought.

In a strong voice, so he could be heard over the roar of the furnace behind him, the short man began, "Good Afternoon. My name is Matt Harris. That's Jared, my assistant. Today, I'm going to be blowing a large, fluted bowl."

And now," he said, walking toward what looked like an umbrella stand, selecting a long, hollow metal pole, "let's get started!"

As he faced the furnace, he filled in some background for the crowd.

"Glassblowing was originally a Roman art, and the set-up you see here—the tools, the furnace, and the glass—has remained largely unchanged, except for some technical improvements, for at least two thousand years. The glass in the furnace is kept at a working temperature of twenty-three hundred degrees. Normally, you have a furnace, then a glory hole in front; but for space considerations, we have combined them here."

The other man slid open the door to the furnace, exposing what looked like the velvety back of a fiery dragon, slowly coiling within. As Matt approached the furnace, hefting the pole, he reminded Logan of a medieval knight approaching the dragon's lair, lance down, ready for battle.

10

Unfazed by being inches away from the ferocious heat, Matt dipped one end of the long pole into the crucible of white-hot, molten glass.

"The first step is to take a gather of clear glass from the glory hole, onto the end of the blowpipe."

The two men moved in comfortable concert, punctuated by Matt's verbal explanations as they worked their way through the process of gathering, blowing out the vase with carefully measured breaths, adding color by rolling it in the chips of glass, reheating it, blowing it out again. They made it look easy.

"The reason we keep putting the piece back in the glory hole is because, if it cools too much the glass is no longer workable. Notice I'm constantly spinning the pipe while it's in there. This is to keep gravity from pulling the piece off center. Sometimes you want that effect; but for this piece, I'm trying to keep the sides even—keep everything centered," Matt said.

"How long did it take you to learn how to become a glass-blower?" came an admiring question from the audience.

"It takes about fifteen years to become a master glassblower. You never 'become' a glassblower, you are always 'becoming' one," Matt answered briefly, keeping his attention on his work. "You have to watch it carefully, you want it to be just hot enough to work; the depth of placement depends on what section you want to work on next."

He was in the zone now and spoke little until the piece was complete. Each reheat and subsequent gather was accompanied by smoothing sessions with a curved pad of newspaper and a wooden tool that looked to Logan like a gravy ladle. He kept both soaking in a bucket of water next to his bench, about ten yards from the furnace.

Paper seemed a strange medium to use with hot glass. Before Logan could ask "What keeps the newspaper from burning or sticking to the glass?" a small woman in the front did.

Matt either did not hear her, or chose not to answer. Instead, he focused on blowing out the glass a little bit more, twisting the pipe slowly between his lips. He continued to shape his piece, keeping a sharp eye on the glass, and finally said, "It just works best."

Jared explained, "We call the layers of wet newspaper 'the rag,' and it cools the surface of the glass so we can shape it."

Matt shot him an irritated look, but it didn't seem to register, or Jared chose to ignore him. Matt pulled another tool, which looked like a gigantic pair of tweezers, out of the bucket of water and used it to press open the mouth of the piece, as he continued to roll the metal pole deftly, back and forth.

Logan still didn't understand why the glass didn't stick to the metal, but she guessed it had something to do with the water it was kept in. The whole process was impressive and sort of mesmerizing. After a few more turns, Matt stood and holding the blowpipe at about a forty-five degree angle down and away from his body, he blew out slowly, with controlled force expanding the glass one last time. He looked at it critically and made his decision.

On cue, Jared stood back and Matt paused, then spread his legs to shoulder width, anchored his stocky body into a fighting stance and, surprising the audience, deftly swung the blowpipe hand-over-hand, like a demented baton twirler, dramatically flaring out the edges of the bowl with every swing. All part of the show.

Dripping in sweat, he seemed very satisfied with the results. Ooohs and ahhhs escaped from the crowd, everyone vying now for a good position in front, to see the finished piece. Logan joined in the scattered clapping, which silenced quickly, as many knew what was coming next.

The last cool trick was getting the beautiful bowl, which was now over three feet wide at the rim, off the pipe, which Matt did easily, releasing it with a single tap on the opposite end. The bowl detached cleanly and sat, calmly confident in its celebrity, spotlighted in the slanting rays of the afternoon sun.

The finished piece was stunning. He had captured the essence of an ocean wave—not tropical turquoise, but colors true to the gray-blue water of the Pacific Ocean just two miles away. The narrow bottom of the bowl was anchored in an almost black, dark kelp green, then powerfully swirled up and out through speckled blues, tossing a thin ribbon of pale green foam off its rim. You could almost feel the ocean spray.

It was difficult to believe the cool, blue glass had been birthed of the roiling, red-orange pool of molten glass in the furnace. Thirty minutes ago, that graceful bowl had only been a few synapses between neurons in the glassblower's brain.

As Jared began cleaning up, Matt wrapped up the demonstration, "If anyone is interested in purchasing this piece, it will be available in the morning. Right now, it needs to go into the annealing oven to cool down gradually. If I left it out, it would cool too quickly and crack, ruining it. We keep the annealing oven at about nine hundred degrees, as opposed to the working area of the furnace, which is about twenty-five hundred. I have several other large pieces like this one back at the booth, different colors, in addition to smaller pieces. Again, my name is Matt Harris."

11

Show over, people began shuffling over to the glassblowers' booths. With only thirty minutes left on her lunch break, Logan followed the crowd, threading her way gingerly through the displays, trying to avoid bumping into anything. She scanned the shelves, looking for something Bonnie might like and was in her price range. There were cards with brief bios for each of the glassblowers, including how long they'd been working at their craft.

She was surprised to learn that Jared and Matt had an equal amount of experience and, although their styles differed, were both quite good. It was ungenerous of Matt not to promote Jared's work too, Logan thought, as well as his own, or mention that he also was a glassblower, not just an assistant.

Elizabeth, Howard's third intern, was the newcomer, arriving just a few months ago in January. She was not new to the art, though. Her card indicated she had been developing her craft for about three years. Before coming west to study with Howard, she'd won an award back east. The young artist was in the back of her booth, talking with a customer.

Not much taller than the first shelf, Logan noticed, but maybe she just seemed that short because she was wiry. Dressed in a neon yellow and black biking outfit, she looked like she could ride sixty miles before breakfast without breaking a sweat. Not an ounce of fat on her.

When Logan walked up, she was talking with a customer.

"We're all trained by Howard Miller, but we each have our own style, which reflects Howard's skill as a teacher. His philosophy is to give us a solid grounding in glassblowing principles and techniques, while exposing us to a variety of other artists' work. Training with Howard is rigorous, but in the end, it will allow those of us who stuck with it long enough true freedom to express ourselves."

Logan thought that sounded like a good teaching philosophy.

The next two sections held Matt and Jared's work. Matt's pieces were large, powerful, tall vases and wide bowls in bold colors. The man's body brought to mind Neanderthals, but she had to admit, the work he produced was graceful and smooth.

Jared's work was a surprise. It wasn't as impressive at first glance, but upon further inspection, demonstrated a wonderful sense of humor. He blew the requisite large bowls and vases, but most of his pieces had cleverly hidden frogs, or slender water nymphs lounging along the rim.

Next to the cash register were a few glass paperweights. They looked childish by comparison and no one seemed to be buying them. Logan couldn't picture any of the glassblowers making those. They looked more at home in Neva's booth.

Logan wound up selecting two pieces from Jared's booth. The first was a long, canoe-shaped sweep of sky-blue glass, edged in yellow, for Bonnie's large dining room table. It looked great by itself or could be used as a fruit bowl. Her second selection was a small, clear glass water pitcher. A tiny elf lay napping in the curve of the handle, his leaf cap pulled low, shading his face. She brought both to the cash register.

SHATTERED

According to her nametag, the young woman manning the cash register was named Leah. Wearing functional vs. fashionable overalls and a loose-fitting t-shirt, as soon as she saw Logan, she placed a frayed, blue satin ribbon in what looked like a Bible and slipped it under the register before ringing up Logan's purchases.

"That will be a hundred and twenty-five for the bowl, and fifty-five dollars for the water pitcher, tax included," she said. Then her eyes sparkled, "Isn't Jared's work great?"

Logan agreed that it was and happily paid with her ATM/ MasterCard, knowing she would have paid twice as much in a department store, and not found anything half so unique or beautiful. Wrapping the bowl first in bubble wrap, securing it with tape, Leah looked under the counter for a large enough bag, but couldn't find any.

"We're out of the bigger bags right now, with the handles, but I'm going to go back to the compound and get some during my lunch. I have a break soon. If you can wait until this afternoon, I can get you a one with carrying handles."

"I work just around the corner, with Thomas and Lisa," Logan said. "I have to get back now, but I can stop by later and pick it up—no problem."

Just then, Jared walked up. Stepping behind the counter, he put his left hand gently between Leah's shoulder blades, rubbing in small circles. He kissed the girl on the top of her head. She immediately brightened, smiling up at him.

"How you doing, hon? Need a break?" Jared offered.

"I'm good," she said.

"Okay, then, I'm going to go grab us some burgers. Fire Fries?"

Leah nodded.

"The works?"

"I'll have whatever you're having," Leah answered.

"Good choice," Logan said.

"Hey," Jared said, "What'd you think of the demo? Isn't Matt good?"

If Jared felt any resentment toward the other man's dismissive treatment of him during the demo, it didn't show. His face remained open and cheerful. They talked a little about the glassblowing process, which Logan found very interesting.

Just then, Elizabeth came in from the booth next door and asked, "You have any change? I've got a woman needs to break a hundred."

Leah opened the cash drawer and pulled out five twenties, holding them out to her.

Elizabeth quickly grabbed the twenties from Leah's hand and handed Jared the hundred-dollar bill.

"Thanks, Jared!" she said, tossing her parting comment over her shoulder as she hurried back to her customer.

Leah began straightening paperweights.

12

Oblivious to Leah's hurt at being snubbed, Jared pointed enthusiastically to the colorful, glass hemispheres she was arranging next to the register.

"Have you seen these? Leah makes them. They have cool hearts and things inside. This one has a daisy in it! You should pick up a few sometime, too. She's an amazing woman, my girl. An artist, the best girlfriend anyone could ask for, AND is going to make a great wife. We're getting married!" he said, holding up Leah's left hand.

Leah blushed. Logan made appropriate oohs! and ahhs! over the slender, gold ring with its microscopic diamond chip perched jauntily on top. From the proud expression on Leah's face, it could have been the Hope diamond.

"And a great mother someday," Jared added, planting another kiss on top of her head.

"I'll have to check those out next time I'm in," Logan said politely, "but I need to get back now. I'm working with Thomas and Lisa," she said to Jared, nodding her head in the direction of their booth, "Do you know them?"

"Not really, but I need to get over there. They seem really nice and they have cool stuff. How do you know them?"

"I knew Thomas back in high school. I'm just helping out for the summer. It brings back old memories. We used to work here every year as kids."

"Well, welcome back to the Otter Festival Family!" Jared said, loping off to retrieve their lunch.

Jared and Leah probably hadn't even been born when she last worked at the Otter Festival in high school. God, she felt old! Watching Jared's bouncing gait, she wondered about their getting married so young, and with no visible means of support. She doubted apprentice glassblowers made much money. From what Thomas had told her, it cost up to twenty thousand for even a simple studio set up.

True to her word, Leah went home and got the bigger bags. She delivered them to Logan that afternoon, waiting patiently, admiring the items in the case, until Logan had finished explaining to a customer that obsidian was really volcanic glass, highly prized by Native Americans for making a variety of tools. According to one study, it could make scalpels sharper than those made of surgical steel.

"Very cool!" gushed the customer, as Logan rang up her purchase. Logan was pleased she was able to answer the woman's questions herself. She was getting good at this!

As enjoyable as the day had been, Logan found herself anticipating the luxury of an evening alone. After locking up the booth and waving to Iona on the way out, she buckled herself into the driver's seat and completed the three-point mirror check her Dad had instilled in her since she was sixteen.

Nosing her car out of the parking lot onto Second Street, she merged onto PCH and headed home. As the Corvette warmed up, taking the curves with power and grace, Logan relaxed. She felt a little guilty about how good she felt. She hadn't thought about Jack all day.

SHATTERED

She read about this zigzag, healing pattern in one of the many self-help books people gave her after Jack died. You were supposed to accept all feelings as they came——good or bad—without judgment. It was the one piece of advice that stuck with her and had proved the most useful. Don't fight the sadness when it comes, just let it wash over you—wade through it, and it passes. And don't fight the joy, either. Being happy doesn't mean you loved the person any less.

Traffic was light and Logan's luck held, because when she got home, her washer and dryer had been delivered.

"Hallelujah and Hail Mary!" Logan announced to Dimebox, who was busy rubbing against her ankles.

The appliances still needed to be installed, so Logan again parked outside in the gravel driveway. After feeding Dimebox, who had been out scouting the neighborhood and wasn't hungry, she checked the cat box and found it had not been used.

"Been tomcatting around, eh?" she pretend-scowled at her no-longer-tiny cat. "You don't know it, but your dating days are numbered, pal. Next week you have an appointment to get snipped. We don't want any paternity suits, you know."

Dimebox ran ahead of her up the stairs.

Checking the bags to make sure nothing had broken on the way home, before putting Bonnie's gifts in the hall closet, she discovered Jared's girlfriend had included something a little extra in the bag with her purchases. A religious tract fell out as she was lifting the bag up onto the top shelf.

"Oh jeez," she groaned, picking it up off the floor. Stamped across the front cover in three-inch bright red type, above the face of an angry Jesus, was a one-word command . . . REPENT! Logan gingerly placed it face down on the counter.

Why did some religions portray God as perpetually angry? Logan remembered going to Bonnie's church once and their idea was very different. Just inside the foyer, on your way into the chapel, they had a big picture of a warm, smiling, kind Jesus surrounded by adoring children. Maybe there was more than one Jesus and Leah just hadn't met the nice one yet.

Oh well, to each his own.

After changing into a pair of yoga pants and an old sweatshirt, Logan went back downstairs. She grabbed a bottle of wine and a glass from the kitchen. Using one of her elbows to open the French doors, she let herself outside. Before mounting the stairs to the roof, she stopped and breathed in the summer smells. Fresh-dug earth around Ben's roses, the sharp scent of juniper. Even the briny perfume of the kelp beds smelled good tonight. A full, ivory moon hung low in a navy sky.

"Ahhh . . . ," Logan sighed.

Not to be left behind, Dimebox made it out before she shut the door and followed her up the outside stairs. Once there, she pulled a soft, green wool blanket out of the bench. She had found it in the garage. The color brightened quite a bit after she got it cleaned. It was plain, but warm and serviceable. She wondered if it had belonged to Meg, or some earlier resident.

She wrapped herself in its thick folds. Dimebox approved. He jumped up onto her lap, turned around one and a half times, then settled into a ball and promptly went to sleep.

For the next hour, Logan allowed herself to just be. Thoughts scurried around her head, but eventually slowed. Soothing wave sounds lulled and she gave herself over to gravity. Her body let go and relaxed into the cushions. Soon warm, cool air refreshing her face, she watched the moon slowly rise over the onyx waves, throwing long silver runners onto the surface of the sea, a glittering path for dreams to follow. Absentmindedly scratching her feline leg warmer behind the ears, a fragile and wonderful sense of wellbeing enveloped her.

It just doesn't get any better than this.

She could almost hear the ghosts of sea otters, floating in huge rafts on their backs, beyond the breakers, napping in the kelp, rocked to sleep in the watery arms of the sea.

As she drifted toward her own sleep, she noticed again the almost-full moon, which had risen higher in the sky. Her younger brother, Rick, a local cop, had warned her once to stay close to home when the moon was full. The department always put on extra patrols then. Full-moon nights were notorious for not just more calls, but stranger ones, particularly incidents of personal violence: lovers, spouses, suicides . . .

She should have checked the calendar.

13

They'd been working since early that morning and Logan's stomach was starting to growl. Grabbing some money from her purse, she volunteered to pick up lunch since Thomas and Lisa both still had customers.

Logan left the booth and began meandering toward the food court, enjoying the chance to stretch her legs. She didn't need to be back before 1:30 p.m., so had plenty of time.

She passed Iona, who was in high spirits, laughing and flirting with a couple of delivery-men who were wheeling a case of soda to the food court. And they were flirting back.

A short rain shower last night washed the dust out of the air, leaving everything fresh and clean. Two booths down the path, Logan stopped to admire a pair of green, sea-glass earrings sparkling invitingly from a clever display rack angled to catch and reflect the sun's rays as customers walked by. She checked to make sure the silver loop was well soldered before trying them on.

"They really bring out your eyes," the woman said as she held up a mirror for her, "Would you like to wear them?"

Logan did, and after paying and putting them on, slipped the silver hoops she had been wearing into the small drawstring silk pouch the woman handed her, and into her pocket. Chin up, head back, she lowered her eyelids to half-mast, turning her head a few times, checking herself out in the mirror that now rested on the counter.

Laughing at her vanity, she tossed her hair back over her shoulder, just for the joy of feeling its soft movement on her neck. As she turned to go, feeling sixteen again, all summery and light, she tripped right into a wall of chest, almost knocking down the man belonging to the chest.

"Whoa," Ben laughed, catching her by both arms in a firm grip to keep her from falling.

Blushing furiously, wondering how much hair tossing Ben had seen, Logan tried to recover quickly.

"Oh, sorry, need to watch where I'm going."

"No worries," he smiled, "that's part of the good neighbor service I provide. It's in the code, actually, section twenty-four, paragraph two.

Tongue-tied, Logan just stood there, frantically thinking of something clever to say.

Ben let her off the hook this time, "Where are you off to in such a hurry anyway?"

"Just going to grab some lunch," Logan replied, glad to change the subject, "What are you doing here?

"I came over to plan some work on Solange's fountain out front."

"Why? What's wrong with it?"

"Nothing with the fountain itself, just some landscaping modifications she's looking at. I need to see if it's something we can do now, or if we need to wait until September, when the fair is closed."

Logan nodded, "Sounds good."

"Well," Ben continued, "I'd better let you get to your lunch."

"Okay. Good luck with your fountain." Logan replied.

She turned to walk in the direction of the food court, grateful he hadn't teased her about her looking in the mirror, admiring herself. She'd dodged that bullet.

But Ben got in the last word, calling after her, "They really do bring out your eyes."

Damn.

Unable to think of a witty response fast enough, she just kept walking.

Putting away two Jasper burgers helped her regain her equilibrium. She still had about forty-five minutes before she had to be back, so she decided to stop by the glassblowers' cage and see if she could catch another demo. So far, she'd only seen Matt do his. She was in luck. She got there in time to see the new girl, Elizabeth, put the finishing touches on a fluted, scarlet vase. An elongated oval narrowing to a delicate neck, topped in a brilliant yellow rim, it reminded Logan of a tropical bird—small, compact, yet exuding strength, like the glassblower herself.

The wiry five-foot-five woman started a new project. Taking a warrior's yoga stance in front of the furnace, balancing perfectly, she looked as if she might pole vault instead of blow glass. In fact, she reminded Logan of an Olympic gymnast: concave stomach, slightly bow-legged, muscular thighs.

Hair pulled up into a neat ponytail left her heart-shaped face open to the searing heat of the glass furnace. She wore a pink bandanna to keep the sweat out of her eyes. Ropy biceps twisted slightly each time she rotated the long metal pole or put it back in the furnace to reheat or gather more glass.

In contrast to Matt, Elizabeth worked silently. Jared, who was assisting again, did all the talking with the audience this time. He didn't seem to mind answering questions and, in fact, enjoyed it, and the crowd enjoyed him. He had just completed a mock bow as she settled in to watch. Leah, his girlfriend, who seemed to be everyone's assistant, beamed at him from the sidelines after replacing the water jug by the door.

Elizabeth's style was as intense as Matt's, although less showy. More precise and controlled. But there was something more. Logan couldn't quite put her finger on it, but watching the young woman work she sensed an underlying hum of desperation, as if Elizabeth fought against time or some unseen foe.

14

When the piece was safely placed in the annealing oven and the poles put back in their racks, Elizabeth stepped toward the exit, pouring herself a glass of water from the jug before emerging from the cage. Lemon slices floated in it. Good idea, Logan thought. Working in front of that oven must take it out of them.

During the last few days, Ned had introduced her around to a few more people, including Howard Miller. Logan was impressed. A well-known and respected glassblower in his own right, Howard could have retired long ago or focused on his own work, which still commanded hefty prices. But he chose to open a glassblowing school instead to mentor new talent, sharing his expertise with the next generation of artists. She hadn't yet been formally introduced to Elizabeth.

Jared recognized Logan right away.

"Hey there! So you got to watch Wonder Woman here at work, eh? Howard says she's the fastest learner he's ever coached," he said.

Elizabeth shrugged off the compliment, but acknowledged it with a nod.

Leah appeared at Jared's side. Giving her a quick squeeze, Jared kissed the top of her head, "Sorry, I'm all sweaty, hon."

Leah handed him a small towel, then went back to their booth to wait on customers.

Logan noticed again how Jared shared the spotlight easily. What a jewel Leah had in him, Logan mused. Very few men were so relaxed and confident. In hindsight, she could see that Jack had hogged the spotlight when they were together, although not with the arrogance Matt exhibited. Jack was just naturally charismatic.

"It was wonderful to watch you work, Elizabeth," Logan said, reaching out to shake her hand.

"Thanks," she responded, wiping her hand on her jeans before gripping Logan's in a firm but brief shake. She reached back into the cage.

"Want one?" She filled another plastic cup and handed it to Logan.

"Thanks."

Logan took a drink and joined the two of them on a nearby bench. For the next ten minutes, Logan sat back contentedly, sipping her water and letting her lunch digest, listening to the two artists discuss how the demo had gone and new techniques they wanted to try. They used terms entirely obscure to Logan, like marvers and jacks, and spent the best part of the next twenty minutes discussing the relative merits of pre-made vs. homemade annealing ovens, and the prohibitive costs of setting up their own shops.

They had just begun to discuss the upcoming glass blowing competition in Finland, when Logan realized it was coming up on 1:00 p.m., time for her to pick up Lisa's Coke and fries and head back to work. She waited for a break in the conversation to say goodbye.

"You could totally do a three-hundred in six minutes!" Jared encouraged Elizabeth.

"The Finn did a two-eighty-one cylinder last year, to win. I just need to practice. I'll get it," she said, without bragging.

"I'll bet if you braced your feet a little wider and crouched—did your warrior yoga thing, and did some weights," he continued excitedly, "you can use our weight bench—it's out in Howard's garage—you could totally break that record! That would be so cool! I'm not going this year."

"Leah and I are getting married," he explained unnecessarily, then turned back to Elizabeth, "but you should totally try. It'd make you a shoe-in for the Chihuly workshop."

She wondered why Jared didn't go for the Chihuly spot himself. From what they'd said, it came with a seven-thousand dollar prize. There seemed to be no anger or competition on his part toward Elizabeth. He was the one about to get married and start a family. She was sure the young couple could use the money.

Maybe he was just what he appeared to be, a nice guy without a mean bone in his body. Those were rare enough finds, male or female. She had to stop being suspicious of everyone!

"Well, guys," she said, standing up and stretching out her stiff right knee, "whatever a three hundred or a two-eighty-one is, I wish you the best with it, and leave you guys to your work. I've got a hungry boss back at the booth."

Logan yawned. She'd pick up two Cokes; she needed some wake-up juice herself after sitting in the warm sun for twenty minutes.

"Sorry," said Elizabeth, and went on to explain, "Two-hundred eight one is how wide the piece is, in centimeters. I'm going to be the first to do three hundred. I just need to get a little stronger. The competition isn't for another month."

She left them making plans to meet up later for a practice session when the cage would be free.

Two other sets of eyes continued to observe them, though, and they were not smiling. One worried; one seethed. Neither onlooker was happy about Jared and Elizabeth meeting that night.

15

"**D**on't tell me you don't know what I'm talking about," a male voice hissed.

"You'd better lower your voice before Howard hears you," came the calm reply.

Logan saw and heard them plainly. She was afraid to move for fear of looking like she was snooping. And well, she was snooping. She'd been taking a shortcut to the back stage through the glassblowers' break area behind the booths when she stumbled onto the combatants. Luckily, they were too engrossed in their argument to notice.

It was Elizabeth and Matt—seated across from each other at a rusty, metal table. A few fast-food wrappers snagged by tufts of dry grass lay scattered around. Tilting her head back, Elizabeth took a long, slow drink from her bottle of water, making Matt wait.

Logan couldn't decide whether to sneak back the way she came or just wait until they were done. She was afraid to step forward or backward for fear of the bark chips making noise, alerting them to her presence. In the end, she decided to just wait it out.

The drama continued.

Elizabeth placed the empty bottle down on the table, rubbing the ridges with her thumb, never breaking eye contact. Matt broke first, jumping out of his seat, angrily slamming his hands down on the table, making it wobble.

If she was surprised by his outburst, or frightened in any way, she didn't show it. She cocked her head slightly to the left, narrowing her blue eyes to laser intensity.

Frustrated, Matt removed his hands as if the table were hot, and took a step back, still facing her.

"You're amazing, you know that?" Matt muttered, scraping his fingers through his thick hair, squeezing his eyes shut.

Suddenly he reached down and with one quick movement, flipped the table onto its side, sending it rolling until it was stopped by a rock, about ten feet away.

"You know what? You can have it! Take whatever you want from whomever you can get it from. We both know you're good at that! Who haven't you screwed?"

Clearly he expected a reaction, but Elizabeth remained seated, considering him in her steady gaze, as if he were a strange, slightly odorous bug.

Matt began to pace, then turned back sharply, righting the table then leaning in until he was inches away from Elizabeth's face, snarling, "I've put in my time, worked for over seven long years to be where I'm at, and no *skank* is going to come in here and take what's rightfully mine by shaking her tits at Howard."

Elizabeth's speech slowed even more, and came back so low, Logan could barely hear her. She leaned in and held her breath.

Enunciating carefully, as if Matt were a child, Elizabeth said, "Listen to me, you gross, smelly, untalented prick. I have more talent in my little finger than you do in your entire, disgusting, hairy body. Internships aren't won by seniority, they're won by skill, and I simply have more than you."

With that, she regally rose from her chair and left the area neatly, without looking back.

"Fuck!" Matt exploded, kicking a nearby orange crate, caving it in on one side, then storming off in the opposite direction.

Logan let out the breath she didn't realize she'd been holding and tiptoed back the way she'd come.

Wow. Who knew glassblowing had so much drama?

After Logan retreated, a second observer exited the supply shed nearby, thoughtfully mulling over this new information.

16

While Logan and the other first arrivals waited, Iona made her way over to the gate, picking up trash as she went, bitching the whole time through Strawberry Sugar lips. Said lips were clenched on her after-breakfast cigarette, which waggled up and down with each new obscenity. She stuffed a mustard-stained wrapper and some empty Coke cans wet with dew into a trashcan. The night security guard was going to get an earful for littering her otherwise pristine grounds.

"It's clean when I leave, I expect it to be clean when I come in," she muttered.

Giving the sign-in table one last check, making sure the clipboards all had pencils, she hauled out a massive key ring from her belt loop, locating the gate key. Miraculously, she didn't break any of her three-inch cherry red nails as she unlocked the padlock and untangled the complicated, tight twist of chain that secured the back gate. Mission accomplished, she waved the waiting vendors in.

"One at a time, one at a time. You, too!" she hollered as Matt sauntered in, bypassing the line.

"Bite me . . . " he grumbled.

Lucky for him, he was out of Iona's earshot before coming over to scribble his name under her disapproving glare. If her hearing was better, Iona would have done a whole lot more than glare. But it wasn't, so Matt escaped her wrath.

Today's hairdo was her standard, lacquered French Twist with a bright yellow bow in the back. Red jeans and checkered Vans completed the outfit. Pulling up her chair, Iona retrieved the ubiquitous pencil from behind her left ear and glowered at each person as they filed past.

Who needed sunshine with Iona around? Iona's grouch routine always put Logan in a good mood. There was something reassuring about her consistency.

Logan signed in, checked the weekly schedule to make sure none of her playing sessions overlapped with her booth schedule, grabbed a coffee from Athena's, then settled in to wait at one of the café tables in the food court for Thomas and Lisa to arrive. The food court was a good fifty feet away from the gate, but she could still see the employee entrance. She'd see them when they came in.

Neva tramped by, dour as ever, loaded down with a couple of old Macy's shopping bags, not stopping to talk to anyone. Rose, the weaver, wearing one of her long, knit vests in mossy greens and rusts, took the far right path. Walking next to the stream, the sun glinting off her steel gray hair, she looked like one of Tolkien's massive tree spirits.

Howard Miller's angular, white-thatched, six-foot-four frame contrasted with Elizabeth's petite form walking next to him. Deep in conversation, there was a gentleness to the way he pulled back his long strides to match her shorter ones, bending down to catch whatever she was saying.

Thomas and Lisa still hadn't arrived, but it was a beautiful day. Logan didn't mind the wait. Several more vendors signed in, none of whom she recognized, but the next face was a familiar one. At a petite 5'2," Glenda Evans looked more forest sprite than tree goddess. She had been the school nurse when Logan was growing up.

Glenda spotted her and came right over.

"Logan McKenna! It has been too long. I was really sorry to hear about your dad. He was such a good father to you guys. Never missed a parent/teacher conference or Back to School Night. And then Jack. You've had quite the last few years. How are you doing? You okay?"

There was no small talk with Glenda.

"Thank you, Glenda. I'm fine, really. Thank you for asking. What are you doing here?"

"Oh, I retired. This is my second year at the fair. I decided since I was growing all those herbs anyway, and people kept asking for them, I'd set up shop and make some money off it! I'm working on an herb book, too."

Logan congratulated her on her new venture and for the next few minutes they philosophized and caught up over another cup of coffee. Glenda had her own thermos of tea. Logan filled her in on the sale of the computer business, buying the house, adopting Dimebox, and her tentative beginnings at teaching, ending with the threatening letter from Metterson.

Due to her long-running employment in the district, Glenda knew Logan's principal well.

"Metterson's a small man, a bully." Glenda said, "Watch your back, though. He's an idiot, but an idiot with friends."

"I'll keep that in mind," Logan replied, wishing she didn't have to think about him at all.

"Well, don't worry about it now," Glenda got up briskly. "These things have a way of working themselves out. I'd better get going. Come by the stand and I'll give you some catnip for your new kitty."

Logan promised, although she didn't know what catnip was, or why Dimebox might want it.

17

It was all fine and well to get up early for work, but to do so voluntarily on a beautiful, Sunday morning was something else. Logan instantly regretted having agreed to troop down to Tava'e's with Ben so early. Only the thought of a lethal injection of caffeine got her out of bed.

"Mmmmphhhh!" she groaned in muffled protest into her pillow.

Ben promised to help Rick, her little brother by four years, carry in an old steamer trunk she planned on using as a coffee table. It had been out in the garage while the wood floors were being refinished. Knowing Rick, he'd be early.

Dimebox, who'd earned his right to sleep on the bed after demonstrating perfect continence five days in a row, yawned widely and stretched in a half-moon arch, then pulled back into a ball. He continued to sleep, blissfully unconcerned, while Logan dragged herself out of bed and hit the shower.

True to his Scandinavian word, Ben was on her doorstop, the faithful Purgatory by his side, at 7:00 a.m. sharp, wearing an old Chapman University sweatshirt, khaki shorts, and tennis shoes so old and threadbare she didn't see how they could stay on his feet. A huge, calm animal, looking like a handsome mix between a St. Bernard and a lab, Ben informed her Purgatory was a Greater Swiss Mountain dog his grandparents had given him as a puppy.

She was just about to call Rick and have him meet them down at the café for a cup of coffee first, before his shift, when he pulled up in his patrol car behind Lola.

While Logan got the long, lean build, Scotch-Irish auburn hair and fair skin, Rick took after their mother's Southern European side of the family. Black-haired, black-eyed, olive-skinned and stocky, he was only taller than Logan if he stood up really straight—which he always tried to do. Slightly insecure about his height, he made up for it with a rigorous weight-lifting schedule. Giving his sister a hug, he turned back to let his partner out of the car.

"Hey, Charlie," Logan said in greeting, scratching her behind the ears.

Charlie was a long, lean German Shepherd—all shoulders, no hips. Born in Bulgaria, trained here in the US, she and Rick had worked together for about two and a half years. Charlie was a real bitch, but only to the bad guys.

Rick's first dog, Zeus, was killed during a drug bust. He didn't want to lose another partner, and wasn't convinced the war on drugs was worth the manpower and lives it cost, anyway. It seemed to put all the wrong people in jail. Junkies and low-level dealers crowded California's jails, while the top guys just kept raking in the money.

After he lost Zeus, Rick asked to be reassigned—anything but the drug unit. A true "Jaws and Paws" K-9 partner, Charlie was more focused on chasing down robbery and assault suspects than sniffing out drugs. Rick liked it that way.

When Charlie looked at you, the first thing you noticed, besides her size, was her eyes. Depending on whether her partner identified you as friend or foe, they looked out from her alert face with warmth and intelligence or turned into two burning lasers trained on your throat. Her graceful walk belied the strength and speed for which she was known. Once Rick gave the command, Charlie took off like a bullet. No suspect had outrun her yet.

Currently, those eyes looked up at Logan with soft warmth, and leaned in for more of those delicious ear scratches, which weren't hard to deliver, as her head came up to Logan's waist. Charlie knew she was off-duty, and happily trotted after Logan into the living room, leaving Rick to shut the door. Dimebox retreated to the upstairs bedroom. No fan club there.

Rick followed them in and sat down on Logan's new saddle-brown leather couch. They'd delivered it last week. It was a fold out couch so Amy would have someplace to sleep when she visited. It had taken three workmen to carry it in through the French doors in back. That thing was solid. Logan believed in good furniture that lasted.

It almost filled the small living room, topping an oval Persian rug, woven in richly muted reds and greens. Well, for the price she paid it probably wasn't a real Persian rug, but it was soft, warm, and thick enough to dig her toes into, which she did on a daily basis. Charlie must have agreed, because she quickly commandeered a spot in front of the couch.

Logan was still deciding whether or not she could afford the gorgeous, handmade rocking chair she'd seen her first day at the festival. She had the cash; she just didn't know if she'd need it come fall if she didn't go back to Tilcott.

Possibly-soon-to-be-out-of-work teachers shouldn't be buying handmade rocking chairs that cost almost a month's salary. On the other hand, if she wasn't working, she'd have plenty of time to sit in it, so she might as well spring for the best.

Rationalizing was a wonderful talent to have.

Ben reached out to shake Rick's hand. Logan made introductions as he joined them on the couch. Purgatory was making his own introductions to the lovely Charlie. After looking Ben over evenly, Rick's brother radar seemed satisfied and he let down his guard a teensy bit.

Nodding toward Ben's house next door, he said, "Nice place. Logan says you're a landscape guy."

Charlie was just beginning to return Purgatory's overtures when Rick's radio receiver, which was clipped to his shirt, crackled on.

"Frank-Ninety-Nine dispatch . . . Frank-Ninety-Nine dispatch"

Rick responded, "Frank-Ninety-Nine."

"Possible one-eighty-seven at Jasper Otter Festival, glass-blowers' cage in the center of the grounds."

In less than a minute, Rick was back in his patrol car, buckling in, with Charlie sitting at attention, ears up and ready to roll. Purgatory looked disappointed.

"Security will meet you at the back gate. Handle code three," Logan heard the dispatcher inform him over the radio as he backed out onto the street.

"Sorry, Sis!" Rick called out his window.

Within forty-five seconds, Rick's black and white hurtled down Killer Hill and turned left onto PCH, lights on, siren wailing. From every cop show she'd ever seen, Logan knew that a 187 meant a homicide. But who was dead, and how could anyone in the sleepy town of Jasper get themselves murdered?

18

Logan didn't have a TV, so Ben went home to see if he could find anything on the news while she called Thomas and Lisa to see if they knew anything. She and Ben agreed to meet up later.

Lisa, who'd been up late working on her powwow dress for the next weekend, answered the phone, sounding groggy. She said Thomas must already be up and went to get him. She found him in the backyard, where he'd been working on a project, and handed him the phone.

Neither of them knew any more than Logan did. There didn't seem to be anything she could do until she heard from Rick or it showed up on the news.

Wired and really needing a run, Logan settled for scrubbing the shower instead, so she'd be near her home. Her cell didn't always get good reception on the beach. Her mind kept spinning with the news.

It hadn't hit her at first, but the idea of someone possibly being killed just a few yards away from Thomas and Lisa's booth seemed so unreal. Maybe the person was just injured. They said glassblowing was dangerous, but these guys knew what they were doing and must have safety procedures in place to protect them, right? And who would have been there before the festival opened for the day, anyway? Was it one of the glassblowers? Did glassblowers work early?

Or maybe another person entirely. One of Iona's security people? A break-in? Maybe Rick would call and say the dispatcher got it wrong, and whomever it was, was okay. She didn't know when he'd be able to call. After all, this was his job, and his job wasn't to keep her updated. She scrubbed harder. She'd just started in on the floor when her cell rang.

"Logan, Rick. I just have a few minutes . . . "

"Okay, but who got hurt? Are they okay?"

"No, they're not okay. A young girl, one of the glassblowers, Elizabeth something. One of the other glassblowers, Matt, came in early and found her this morning."

"That's terrible. What happened?"

"They don't know much yet . . . probably a jealous boyfriend or something. But I wanted to let you know Lisa will probably be calling you any minute."

"Lisa? Why?"

"I want you to listen to me," he spoke very clearly.

"Is Lisa okay?" Logan's voice rose in alarm. She hated it when Rick used his 'big brother' voice. As if . . .

"Thomas and Lisa are fine, but I want you to listen for a minute. There is no reason to worry, but they are bringing Thomas in for questioning . . . "

Logan struggled to remain calm and not interrupt.

"Are you there?" Rick asked.

"Yes, I'm here—I'm here! Why do they want to talk to Thomas?" she managed to get out.

"Iona says she saw him. Said he was here earlier this morning."

"But he was . . . I just talked to them this morning. Thomas was home."

"Did he say he'd been there all morning?"

"Well, no, I didn't ask him that."

"Did anyone besides Lisa see him?" asked her brother, the cop.

Logan remembered Lisa was sleepy when she answered the phone. She did not volunteer the fact that Lisa had not actually said she'd seen Thomas earlier that morning, or that Thomas had neglected to mention that he had been at the festival that morning.

"This is ridiculous. Iona doesn't open up until 9:00 a.m."

"Well, she says she saw him, Logan. Iona doesn't lie. If she said she saw him, she saw him."

Logan could think of nothing to say. If there was one thing Iona was, it was honest. Her mind desperately searched for reasonable explanations.

Why hadn't Thomas mentioned he'd been at the festival this morning?

"Look, I've got to get back. The Detective's on his way, but there's a big accident just north on PCH. That's why Charlie and I got called. It'll take him a while, and the ME maybe two or three hours to get here, so we need to stay put until then. If you talk to Lisa, tell her not to worry. They just have to talk to everyone who was there anywhere close to the time the woman was killed. They'll talk to everyone that was here. Iona went down to give her statement, too. I'll call you as soon as I can.

"Stay home, Logan," he added.

"Call when you can," Logan said, disconnecting before he could hear her car keys jingle as she grabbed them off the hook.

19

Scrambling under dry brush and scrub oak along the side of the hill that formed the natural backdrop of the festival, Logan slowly worked her way down to a spot behind the maintenance shed, which was flush against the chain-link fence. The maintenance area allowed easy access to the stages, plumbing, storage and electrical boxes. It was also the perfect place for getting a closer look. Yellow crime scene tape had already been placed around the glassblower's cage and surrounding booths.

Sharply aromatic eucalyptus trees and thick bushes formed kind of a natural tunnel, making her hiding place all but invisible. The path leading to the maintenance shed was higher here. No one could see Logan, but she could look between the branches of a lemonade berry bush straight into the glassblower's cage and most of the surrounding sawdust-strewn ground.

The familiar plant sparked a family memory. When their mom had left, their dad started taking them on camping trips. On one of their hikes, he had showed her and Rick how to put the lemonade berry seeds into their canteens to make the water taste fresh. She reached up and popped one in her mouth. Yep, still tasted lemony!

Thomas and Lisa's booth was just yards away.

She scanned the area and spotted Rick and Charlie immediately. They were on the farthest side of the cage. Rick was checking his watch, filling out some kind of paperwork on a clipboard, too busy to notice her . . . she hoped. She reached down and made sure her phone was on silent in case he decided to call. She hoped Charlie wouldn't give her away.

She'd have to wait until later to talk with Rick. She didn't see Thomas anywhere, but then they'd probably take him to a police station to question him. Hopefully she'd be home by the time he was done.

In the meantime, she tried to get comfortable, hunkered down on her heels to wait and see what she could see. She didn't yet know what she was looking for, but any bit of information might help.

Hidden by low branches and dense brush, she wasn't more than thirty feet from the large glassblowers' cage but did not worry about being seen. She just had to be quiet so she wouldn't be heard. The forty-by-forty-foot cage being open on all sides, including the top, she could see directly in at about a forty-five degree angle. She settled in to watch and listen.

Everyone seemed to be doing specific tasks, all of which were mysterious to her. A couple of gloved techs finished collecting bits of invisible stuff from the ground and tables with tweezers, placed them into clear plastic baggies. There were already several small bags of litter they'd gathered, tied neatly and leaning along the inside of the cage, next to a gallon jug of water near the door.

Then the wind shifted and Logan was assaulted with a sickening stench of what smelled like overcooked, bad pork. She gagged once, but managed not to throw up.

SHATTERED

Scent memories, connected so directly to our ancient reptilian brains, trigger our strongest emotions. From that moment on, whenever Logan smelled the sharp tang of eucalyptus leaves, like the ones hanging all around her now, her mind would instantly return to the awful sight and smell of the riveting scene below.

Contrasting with the pale, blonde ponytail hanging over the side of the cinderblock box was a black smear of what must have been dried blood. Logan could only see the top third of the body. If there was more blood, it must be inside. The area around the annealing oven—she remembered that's what it was called—was clear, as if no violence had occurred here.

Elizabeth's neck lay unnaturally bent, snapped to one side. The only other thing Logan could see was the top of one jean-clad knee. She hated to think how the rest of her body had been forced to accommodate the walls of the unforgiving space. She recognized it as the annealing oven Matt mentioned in his demo that the glassblowers used to cool their pieces slowly overnight. Who knows how hot the oven still was when the body was placed inside, but obviously hot enough to slowly bake a human body.

Adding insult to injury, the young woman had been shoved directly into the cooling pieces, piercing her back with broken glass. Logan could still see a jagged edge of a large glass bowl jutting out on one side. Hopefully she was already dead before her impromptu burial.

Crime techs continued to mill around the body, like a silent movie. Time seemed suspended. Logan kept wondering why anyone would do this. Interrupting her thoughts, the metal gate to the glassblower's cage clanged. Someone official-looking had arrived.

Logan would later learn he was the Medical Examiner from Orange County. Jasper, being a small town, only had a coroner, and he was on vacation. A former basketball player in his mid-fifties with thinning red hair, the ME bent over Elizabeth's body, causing his belly to strain against his belt.

Logan remembered the annealing oven was temperature controlled, warmer than the outside air, but cooler than the 2500-degree oven of molten glass. After each demo, the glass-blowers carefully placed each completed piece alongside the others, so it would cool slowly and the temperature change would not shock the glass and cause it to shatter.

It was obvious no such great care had been taken with this young woman.

Logan knew she would never get that image out of her mind. The light blonde ponytail looked freshly brushed and neat. She wanted to straighten the body, make her more comfortable, and fix her neck, though she knew the young woman could no longer feel anything.

The ME walked around the body, talking into a tape recorder and to the detectives nearby. Several uniformed officers stood around the perimeter, two EMTs sat nearby, drinking coffee. Waiting.

20

Sound carried in the canyon, but she could only hear parts of what was being said clearly, depending on which way the ME turned his body.

"Rigor mortis passed . . . bloating, streaking, liver temperature . . . stab wounds . . . abdomen . . . extremely sharp . . . You guys find a knife around here? No? Looks deep . . . might be . . . we'll know more when we get her . . . Bad blow to . . . back left. No defensive . . . Probably knocked out first, then stabbed . . . Not a lot of blood . . ."

He paused.

"Whoever did this was pissed. Girl doesn't weigh more than ninety-five to a hundred pounds," he said. "It takes some strength to lift up a dead woman and stuff her into a box like that, even a tiny one like her."

He went back to his work, silently observing the body for a few minutes more, straightening and arching his back while rubbing it.

"What a waste."

He walked over to the taller of the two detectives, who seemed to be in charge.

"Well, that's about all I can do here, Detective . . . Detective . . ."

"Andrews" the man supplied. Logan hadn't noticed him before. He was on par in height with the ME, but with stronger features and black hair. Dark brown pants, leather shoes, nice belt, white shirt, conservative tie. Could have come from church. Do single men still go to church? She didn't see a wedding ring. And why was she looking?

". . . until I get her back to the lab, we're going to have some trouble with the time of death. Even if she hadn't been stuffed into that oven, it's very hot in front of that furnace, and if she'd been standing there a while, blowing glass she would be warmer than usual. Thin, rangy body—these girls are all too skinny if you ask me. Almost no fat. There are a lot of factors. Leaves the window for time of death open a lot wider than I'd like."

"Best estimate?" asked Detective Andrews, scowling at the dead girl, like he could figure out who killed her just by staring hard enough.

"I'll try to narrow it down for you once I run some tests. Right now? Right now, I'd say it could be anytime between around 9:00 last night and maybe six or seven this morning. I'll do the autopsy as soon as I can, but we've got 'em stacked up this weekend, and there's the mess out on PCH. I'll narrow it down for you as soon as I can. Might be as much as a week."

"Do your best," Detective Andrews said.

"At least being this busy gets me out of Sunday dinner at my in-laws," the man added wryly. "My father-in-law could talk your ear off. Knows more than any human being alive about the Civil War. Knows all the battles." He rolled his eyes, "Has maps!" then added cheerfully, as he peeled off his gloves and stuffed them into his jacket pocket, "I'll take work over that any day!"

The young officer standing near the body shifted uncomfortably. He had been standing at parade rest, although no one had told him to, for about thirty minutes, while the ME did his preliminary examination. He would not contradict someone in authority, but obviously felt the old man's comments were disrespectful of the young girl he seemed to have forgotten lay dead at his feet.

In little more than three years' time, this same young man would be eating a ham sandwich not ten feet from a six-car pileup littered with dead bodies, but for now, he still had the innocent's luxury of being offended.

The ME cleared his throat. "Done all I can do here. Okay if we load her up, Detective?"

Detective Andrews nodded his assent and the two men, who had been waiting for the signal, set their paper coffee cups down, stood up and spread a bright blue tarp next to the annealing oven.

Logan expected them to lift the girl reverently, or at least carefully, but she was shocked when they unceremoniously reached in and hauled her out, the body landing with a loud slap onto the tarp. Then they brought the stretcher over and loaded her on.

All this had taken place in no more than a few moments, but Logan felt she'd been rooted to the spot for an hour. Stiff, drained and exhausted, she pushed herself up to a standing position, over the grinding protest of her right knee, which had bothered her since the accident, and worked her way back down the hill.

The dead woman in the box below bore no resemblance to the vibrant, talented glass blower she had seen last week. She had not been the warmest person, but why would anyone want to kill her? No one deserved to die like that.

After she'd made her way back to the beginning of the path, she could hear Iona at the back gate, repeating her instructions and answering the vendors' questions who had gathered at the employee entrance around the corner. Some had arrived before hearing about the murder.

"We're shut down for the rest of the day," Iona barked, "No, you may *not* go back in for anything."

"Yes, that means *you*!" Iona glared at Rose, the weaver, who apparently wanted to go back to her booth to retrieve something. "Sleeping Beauty's spinning wheel sat gathering dust for a hundred years and still worked. Yours can sit there for one day."

In spite of the circumstances, Logan had to smile at the tiny spitfire successfully intimidating the towering Rose, staring her down until she turned and left without a word.

Iona continued, "Officers said we can reopen when they're done. The whole damn place is a crime scene. Go home, now. We'll use the telephone tree to keep you updated. If you do not have a phone, then you may call the main number to reach a recording, which I will make myself, as soon as the officers tell me anything."

"My cash box! My box is still in there!" Neva Schultz had rushed up from somewhere, pleading in a raspy, unused voice. "I . . . I forgot to take it last night. I need to go in."

Logan had rarely heard the woman speak. If Neva left Saturday's cash there for some reason, it would be perfectly safe until tomorrow. There were a dozen cops roaming around. No one was going to get past a dozen cops.

Though, come to think of it, she just had.

Iona spoke to the frightened woman in a sympathetic tone saved for small children and town drunks, "Now, Neva, you know I can't let you in to go to your booth. No one's allowed in right now. I can ask a policeman to walk me back in there, I suppose . . . ," she offered, looking at her watch, turning toward a knot of officers a few yards away.

Neva's blue-veined hand shot out from a dirty, white sweat-shirt sleeve and latched onto Iona's forearm with surprising strength.

Iona turned and stared at Neva, who quickly let go and backed off.

"No, that's okay, Iona. You don't need to get anyone. I'll come back tomorrow. I'm sorry I bothered you," Neva said.

Logan expected Iona to let the woman have it, but Iona surprised her. Eyeing the stooped little woman curiously, she took a long drag on her cigarette, as if something had just become clear.

She spoke in a new, not unkind, level tone. "That's okay, Neva. I understand. You go on home now. Your cash box will be safe here overnight. I'll see to it."

Neva let out the breath she'd been anxiously holding and, without further argument, walked reluctantly to her car, resigned, if not happy, with Iona's solution.

What the hell was going on? What was in her booth that Neva was so anxious to protect, and why had Iona, who didn't even tolerate sideways looks from teenagers, allow Neva to get away with grabbing her arm like that? Normally, Iona shot down anyone who entered her air space, let alone touched her!

Nothing was making sense. Nobody was acting normal today. Maybe it was the full moon. Last night she remembered seeing it, a luminous Japanese lantern hanging precariously off the Big Dipper.

21

Having seen what she could see, learning nothing, Logan drove home. About an hour after she got back, Lisa called to let her know Thomas was on his way home too. The police just wanted to know why he was there and if he knew the murdered girl. He'd explained he only knew her in passing. He went down to their booth that morning because he wanted some quiet time to work before the festival opened. The security guard knew him and let him in, and that was verified.

Logan wanted to ask Lisa if she knew he had gone into the festival, and if so, why she hadn't mentioned it that morning, either, but decided as long as Thomas was home and safe, that's all that mattered.

The police must have accepted his explanation, because they let him go, along with Matt, the glassblower who discovered the body when he came in to set up, Iona, and the night security guard. They had all been on the grounds.

What was it they always said? *Opportunity, Means, and Motive.* They'd all had the opportunity, but nobody had a motive. For now, Rick told her, the police didn't have a suspect, but it was still early in the investigation. Something would turn up.

Finishing up the shower, Logan decided to tackle some weeds in the front yard. It was almost 4:00 p.m. before she came in, looked at a clock and realized she hadn't eaten all day. She felt shaky, either from low blood sugar or delayed shock at seeing Elizabeth's body, she wasn't sure. She was just rummaging in the fridge for something to eat when Ben showed up at the back door with provisions. She opened the French doors and let him and the delicious smell of warm bread, in.

"Sorry, Ben. I meant to call you and fill you in on what's happening since Rick peeled out of here this morning."

"No worries. Saw you out in the yard and thought you might need some food."

"Thank you! Your timing is perfect," she said.

While polishing off the ham sandwich on hot, crusty pretzel bread slathered in spicy mustard he'd made for her, Logan spent the next hour filling Ben in on what she knew, which wasn't much. She even told him about her foray onto the festival grounds. Ben proved to be a good listener.

After she finished eating, they climbed the stairs to the roof with the rest of the cold beer Ben had included in his care package, and settled into the chairs. She felt momentarily guilty for enjoying the sandwich and looking forward to watching the sunset with Ben, as if it were disrespectful to the dead, even though she knew that didn't make sense. For a few minutes, neither spoke. Logan was the first to break the silence.

"I still can't believe it. She was about Amy's age, Ben."

Ben scooted his chair next to hers. The afternoon on-shore breeze grew cool, and they sat side by side, watching the ocean for a while.

"If she has family here, if there's a service, I want to go to it." Then she surprised herself by asking, "Will you come with me?"

Ben nodded his assent, covering their laps with the wool blanket Logan kept in the little trunk she'd hauled up to keep pillows and other rooftop essentials dry and took her hand in his. It felt good.

22

As she turned up Killer Hill, Logan tapped the gold wedding ring she still wore lightly against the steering wheel. Afternoon sunlight glinted bright gold off the windows at Tava'e's. Her thoughts turned to her evening with Ben. He'd left around midnight. Maybe she should have asked him to stay. No. Too soon. Maybe never. What was she doing starting something with a neighbor?

Logan forced herself to think of other things, besides what Ben might look like naked. Home improvement projects seemed safe. Conveniently, her to-do list was very long, even though she'd been gone all day doing errands. Seemed an appropriate way to spend a Monday.

Returning home, she passed the coffee shop. Bright blue awnings shaded the large picture windows from the afternoon sun. After Tava'e's was an empty lot deemed too narrow to build on. The city was still debating its future. Next came a consignment shop for twenty-somethings. It carried every-thing she had gotten rid of in the eighties. The next two properties were residential, small pre-war houses with shallow lawns and deep roots that buckled the sidewalks.

Then came her place. Thanks to Bonnie's gardener—borrowed for a day to pull out years of accumulated debris, both manmade and natural, from around the foundation—it looked like a well-scrubbed child, eager to please. A profusion of morning glories, closed for the day, rambled along the fence. The gardener wisely left those untouched. She turned into the rutted drive and pulled up to the sagging garage. Slanting shadows stole across the yard.

Walking to her front door, she visualized a scattering of stepping stones, maybe with moss growing in between, like those cool-looking gardens in *Sunset* magazine; but hadn't the faintest idea how to do that. Maybe that should be her next project. She'd ask Ben for some ideas. Thinking of Ben now, she certainly had a few . . .

Get a grip, Logan!

Dimebox arrived just in time to distract her thoughts and curled around her legs, purring for all he was worth.

The contractor was pretty much done doing the major projects her dwindling bank account could afford. The rest would have to wait. For now, she'd just enjoy what she had. And what she had right now, she thought as she got out of her car, was the place to herself.

She let herself in, Dimebox trotting behind. The entryway immediately jogged left about seven feet and opened onto an open living and dining area. Full-length French doors at the end led to the back yard. To the left of the doors, in the corner, was a functioning rock fireplace. The kitchen was opposite the French doors, on the other side of the wall dividing it from the entrance, with a small, but sunny window. She'd installed a half bath in what used to be a walk-in pantry in the back of the kitchen.

The solid feeling of the place welcomed her. Small enough to be cozy, airy enough not to be claustrophobic. Opening the kitchen window and the back doors, an ocean breeze immediately whipped through the living room.

She put down her purse, kicked off her shoes and, with a little shiver of joy welling up inside at the pure ecstasy of being free for the summer, did a gleeful Tom Cruise sock slide down the hall.

After years of linoleum and crusty carpet, she savored every inch of this new luxury of hardwood floors. She and Jack put all their money into the company, promising themselves they'd buy a house someday, but there was always a new computer system or marketing campaign to pay for. Her contractor discovered the burnished cherry-wood floors when he'd replaced a section with wood rot. Only one spot needed to be replaced; otherwise, they were in great shape.

Sunlight reflected off the hillside, filtering through the beveled panes, creating a layer of warm, yellow light on the rug. She only had a few pieces of furniture so far. In fact, the only furniture upstairs was her bed, and a nightstand Bonnie gave her.

Enjoying the break from the black-and-beige, ultra-modern décor Jack had preferred, she wanted real things around her. Real wood, real plants, real art. She couldn't wait for winter, so she could have a fire in a real fireplace while she played Bella or curled up in a corner to read a good book. Carl Sagan, C. S. Lewis, Langston Hughes . . . She couldn't wait to fill the built-in bookshelves upstairs with poetry by Rumi or one of her favorites, Benjamin Huff's *The Tao of Pooh*. She was tired of being temporary.

Although many of her goals had been met, she had lots of boxes left to check. Her wish list would have to wait until tomorrow, though. Tonight, she needed to hit the shower and make it to Juan's to meet Bonnie in . . . yikes! She had less than thirty minutes.

23

Juan's was an institution. The grease embedded in the walls could have fueled a small country for at least a year. The interior was lined with tacky Tijuana hats, serapes, and drolly crossed maracas. Outside, in spite of the many plastic owl guardians staked on the roof, it was plastered with seagull shit, which only added to the ambiance as far as Logan was concerned. Kept away the soccer moms.

Only people interested in serious Mexican food came to Juan's, and only a few brave souls made it past the doubtful interior to discover the awesome deck out back.

Those who did were rewarded. Juan's menu was limited, but the food was great. No fake anything and he only served Coke, beer, and strong margaritas. Everything dripped in the freshest grease and if you could completely polish off the infamous "Juan's Two-Die-For" platter, a combination of two chili rellenos, two cheese enchiladas, two chimichangas, two tacos, AND rice, beans and tortillas, your picture went up on the wall behind the cashier with the five other people who'd accomplished the feat in the last ten years. Rick was one of the five. The girl he'd been trying to impress married someone else.

Logan parked a few spaces down and went inside, where working-class couples, seniors, and young families filled the booths.

Her boots made solid sounds on the old plank floor. Turning sideways to get past a busy food server, she made her way through the narrow aisle, past the bar, and out a door propped open with a chair. No spindly cocktail chairs out here. You hunkered down in ancient wooden chaise lounges with faded canvas pads, with wide arms with drink holes, surrounding a big brick fire pit. Regulars learned to bring several layers and add them as the sun went down and the breeze kicked up.

She commandeered a couple of chairs with the fewest rips, near the fire. Saving one for Bonnie, she put her boots up on the outside edge of the fire pit and got comfortable.

Stretching out, Logan rested her eyes on the sea. It was delicious to just sit there, the last rays of the sun warming her face, anticipating a pleasant evening with her friend.

While she waited, she thought about one of Bonnie's well-intentioned neighbors who invited her to meet for drinks at Burton's, a popular oyster bar, a couple of weeks ago, in an attempt to get her to 'get out more.'

She had no desire to get out more. She still felt married, but after they asked several times, Logan had reluctantly agreed.

The scene that greeted her when she walked in confirmed her worst suspicions. A sea of highlighted blondes with boob jobs flirted with a clutch of Ken dolls at the bar. After an obligatory glass of overpriced Chardonnay with Bonnie's friend, Logan made polite murmuring noises and fled.

A familiar voice rescued her from the unpleasant memory of her failed foray into the singles scene.

"Hey, Stranger!" Bonnie could be heard for miles out to sea. She gave Logan a hug, then did a little victory wiggle with outstretched arms, squeezed her eyes shut and crowed, "TGIF!"

After toasting her friend's dancing prowess, and not correcting Bonnie's day-of-the-week skills, the server took their drink order. The sun blazed a final path across the ocean, the air cooled quickly, and Logan could feel the salt settling on her skin. The heat from the fire felt good. Things had been so hectic, this was the first time Logan had time to sit down and spend some time with her friend.

Bonnie was leading a two-week, Summer Reading Academy and had great stories about her students. Unfortunately, talking about school made Logan's year from hell come roaring back. Well, the year was good, but that last day qualified.

Margarita in hand, purse tucked under her chair, Bonnie said, "Okay, spill it. Tell me *everything*!"

Logan fished the letter out of her purse, where it had sat for the last few weeks, unfolded it, smoothed it and passed it to Bonnie, who gave it her full attention, then looked up in amazement.

"Unbelievable! I didn't think even Sheila could stoop this low. She used to work at our school, you know. No one misses her," she said.

"Found it on my desk the last day of school."

Feeling the need for further fortification, Logan flagged down the busy but efficient server, "We'd like some nachos—extra cheese, more salsa and a side of guacamole, and . . . " Logan raised her glass, "another one of these."

"You got it!" the waitress said, maneuvering smoothly through the obstacle course of chairs and fire pits, picking up two more orders on her way back to the kitchen.

"He called me a 'loose cannon'. Think I'll put that on my license plate."

Bonnie laughed, "Now I know what to get you for Christmas!"

"If I don't quit first."

Logan closed her eyes and leaned her head back.

Bonnie's expression turned serious. "I'm sorry I got you into this, but don't quit."

She took another sip of her drink, leaning forward. "You can beat this. You're what those kids need, not more Sheilas. God, save us from the Sheilas!"

"Hear, hear!" Logan clinked glasses and, feeling better, smiled at her friend's rant, grateful for the support.

Bonnie let out a huff and fell back into her chair.

Logan shifted her stiff legs and for a while they sat in companionable silence, comforted by the crackle of the fire, watching the darkening, blue-green sea absorb the molten sun.

The main restaurant was humming now. The happy-hour crowd had gone inside and pulled the door shut, so they were alone on the patio. All quiet, but for the shushing of the waves.

Logan spoke first. "Don't worry. If I want to teach, I'll teach, here or somewhere else."

Bonnie raised her glass, "That's the spirit!"

They decided to order dinner and spent the rest of the evening talking about Mike and the girls' upcoming Disney cruise, and Amy's adventures in Kenya. Bonnie and Mike were also going on a second honeymoon to Puerto Vallarta while her mom watched the kids. No grass grew under Bonnie's feet.

It was almost 10:00 p.m. when, stuffed from all the nachos, Logan patted Lola on the hood, undid the top button of her jeans, exhaled a satisfied sigh, and slid behind the wheel. Her to-do list was already larger than those seventy-six white squares on her calendar, which were now down to what . . . fifty-six? Too much tequila made math impossible.

She couldn't have made it through the last two years without Bonnie's infectious laugh. Her and Mike's open-armed welcome into their home and family could never be repaid. Whatever Logan decided to do about Metterson's letter, it was good to know Bonnie had her back. What would she have done after the accident without her? What did people do who had no family or friends to help during a crisis?

24

Rehearsal had not gone well.

Missed cues, a broken string, and a general feeling that she was playing in a vat of molasses wearing rubber gloves left Logan feeling completely disconnected from her instrument. It was muggy, it was hot, and she was beyond frustrated. Luckily, only the other vendors could hear her.

The glassblower's cage was no longer wrapped in yellow crime scene tape, but neither had the festival reopened. Out of respect for Howard, Solange wanted to wait another week. She would have closed it for the season if so many people didn't depend on summer sales for their winter income.

Ned was being very nice about it, but Logan wondered if he regretted his decision to invite her to fill in for Sal. It had been so long since she really practiced. She hated the thought of disappointing either one of them. And she needed the money.

She couldn't remember when she'd stopped playing her violin, but it was sometime during those first few years of the business. When Amy was a baby Logan played her to sleep every night. It was a special time for both of them.

But when the business started taking off, she was often handling customer support calls with customers in Taiwan and other parts of Asia late into the night. When Logan could tear herself away from work she was picking up groceries for dinner, cooking, catching up on laundry, and getting Jack ready for the next trip. Her beloved violin just kept getting pushed further and farther, literally and figuratively, to the back of her closet.

She and Ned decided to take a break. The food court had been allowed to open a few hours every day for Iona's crew and the artists. After a Greek salad and a glass of Sauvignon Blanc for Logan and a Sam Adams and kabobs for Ned, they walked back and stepped up on the wooden stage. Taylor arrived with his upright bass, so they decided to run through the whole set. Logan loved this stage. The broad, uneven oak planks probably hadn't been replaced since she played in high school, but Logan preferred old and real to new and shiny any day.

Ned swallowed the last of his beer and said, "Shall we?" "Ready if you are," Logan said, with more enthusiasm than she felt.

By the time they'd worked their way through their first few numbers, she felt much better. An onshore breeze freshened the air and sent scraps of clouds scuttling across the low hills behind them. Finding her rhythm, she played off Taylor's bass and Ned's mandolin. The boundaries separating her from the music melted away.

Her fingers flew, and when they got to "Tamylyn's Reel," which starts out with a stroll in A-minor and builds to a joyful climax, everyone within earshot whooped their approval. How could she have lived so long without this joy?

Wiping the sweat from his forehead with an old mechanics rag he kept on top of the speaker, Ned chortled, "You're BA-ack!"

Flushed and happy, she accepted the compliment.

Looking down, Logan was surprised to see Ben, sitting at one of the middle tables, Purgatory asleep at his feet.

She was glad to see him, but it was a little unsettling. How long had he been there? And how did he get in? He wasn't a vendor, but, she remembered, he was friends with Solange. He'd probably been working on the fountain out front.

She waved her bow in recognition, then focused on the music, trying to regain her equilibrium. Ben, on the other hand, looked very relaxed, nursing a beer through the last number, feet stretched out in front of him, scratching Purgatory behind the ears, like he had all the time in the world.

Was he there to see her? Each time he reached down to pet the dog, the muscles in his forearm moved and gave Logan a little tug in her lower regions.

No more wine with dinner for you!

Logan wasn't sure she wanted to start anything right now, especially with a neighbor. That is, if he was there to see her. Was he? She wasn't sure. They stopped for a short break.

Although friendly enough to her, Ben talked mostly to Ned and Taylor. He knew Taylor from using him sometimes on landscaping jobs. In keeping with the musician's lot in life, Taylor wasn't fully employed anywhere. He took any odd job that wouldn't interfere with his music. He lived to play. Did a lot of studio work in Los Angeles. He was also a cowbell wizard.

She spotted several other vendors, too. Jared, his arm around his girlfriend, Leah, still wearing her overalls, sat at one table, and Matt, one of the other glassblowers, was standing in line for a beer.

After the remainder of the set, Ben visited with Taylor about a job for a while, then woke Purgatory from his light coma under the table and headed out with the last of the vendors.

"Hmmm . . . ," Logan muttered to herself, lifting her chin slightly into the air, watching him walk away, "I'm not sure I like that man's attitude."

She didn't have much time to think any more about Ben though because Iona was hustling them out. Iona liked to be at Mullies, the local biker bar by 11:00 p.m., where her evenings really began.

God bless her stamina.

25

"You got everything? Mrs. Whitehorse's dress?" Lisa called to Thomas, who was already in the van.

They'd been informed by Iona's phone tree that the festival wouldn't reopen until at least Monday or Tuesday and the memorial service for Elizabeth wasn't until the following weekend. Lisa had several obligations to attend to at the powwow, so she needed to be there. When they invited her along, Logan happily accepted their offer. Ben originally planned to come, too, but he needed to finish up work on Solange's recycled water project.

Getting out of town was a great idea. They all needed to shake off the gloom that had been hanging over everyone since the discovery of Elizabeth's body. Rick said the detectives were following up on several leads, but still had no viable suspect.

When she got there, the front door was open, so Logan walked back to the kitchen, where Lisa was staring intently into the refrigerator, an open ice chest behind her on the floor.

"Do you think I should throw in some more Cokes?" Lisa said. "I've got room."

Logan looked into the cooler, which was stuffed to the gills. "You've got enough food in there to make it across the Mojave," she told her friend, "I think you're good."

"Doesn't hurt to be prepared," Lisa said, adding a few more cans before shutting the lid and rolling the cooler out to the van. Thomas made no comment about how heavy it was when he lifted it into the back.

The powwow was only an hour and a half away. They would arrive in plenty of time to check in at the motel. The sun warming her shoulder through the window, Logan settled in for the drive.

"Ever had fry bread, Logan?" Lisa asked, turning halfway around in her seat.

"No, I don't think so, but I'm up for anything. I want the whole powwow experience," she said.

"Fry bread is another one of those really unhealthy, 'traditional' foods that became traditional only because once we were stuck on reservations, we couldn't hunt and live off the land like we used to. It's basically white flour, salt, and baking powder, deep fried in lard, but *really* good!"

For the next hour and a half, Lisa gave Logan a basic description of the powwow dances and events. Thomas was content to drive.

They arrived at the San Bernardino Travelodge in time for lunch. Logan put away a generously stacked BLT and fries, while Thomas devoured a full pot roast dinner, complete with gravy and rolls.

Where Thomas put it all, she could not imagine. Lisa did her share of damage to a ham sandwich, and they all had dessert, which consisted of their choice of fresh fruit pies:

peach, strawberry, or boysenberry. Logan chose peach and was glad she did.

"I'm going to have to pace myself," she told herself, walking back across the street to the motel. "Salads . . . more salads."

Before Logan could unlock the door to her room, Lisa hurried toward her, holding out a Safeway bag with a selection of Reese's Pieces, popcorn, freshly baked cookies, and a couple of apples.

"Just in case you get hungry. You never know."

"Have you no mercy?" Logan groaned.

But she took the bag and found room for some of the Reese's Pieces while watching *I Love Lucy* reruns later that night.

They all turned in early. Lisa wanted to be at the main gate when it opened.

*****

The day dawned hot and clear. It had been a while since Logan had been inland, and now she remembered why. She wasn't tough enough to live here. They always said it was a "dry heat," but heat was heat. Anything over a hundred was too hot for human habitation.

The rusty, metal thermometer on the pole outside her room read ninety-one degrees and it was only 8:15 a.m.

Thomas and Lisa had ordered breakfast by the time Logan slipped into the booth at the diner. The server brought her a mug, poured her some coffee and asked what she wanted. She was briefly tempted by the boysenberry pancakes, but remembering her pacing promise, ordered a fruit bowl.

The waitress hesitated, pencil poised over the pad.

"The prairie scramble's good," she dispassionately advised.

"No, I'm not that hungry," Logan lied.

"Suit yourself."

Ten minutes later, the waitress came back, expertly balancing two heavy platters on her left arm and hand.

In front of Thomas, she delivered a chicken-fried steak the size and shape of Texas, so big it hung over the sides of his plate. Smothered in creamy, country gravy, it shared real estate with at least a pound of crispy hash browns, framed by three flaky biscuits.

Next, the waitress deposited a towering, golden stack of buttermilk pancakes with a container of four syrup selections in front of Lisa.

In front of Logan, she plunked a shallow bowl of anemic watermelon chunks and slimy green melon slices.

"I tried to steer you straight," the waitress muttered as she ambled back to the register to ring somebody up.

Thomas chuckled. Lisa offered to share her buttermilk pancakes.

"I can't eat this much before I dance anyway," Lisa said, her eyes bright with excitement.

Logan relieved her of two of the monster pancakes, pushing the fruit bowl discretely aside.

"Okay, explain again what I'll be seeing, and what you're going to be doing. Thomas never taught me about any of this stuff."

"That's because I didn't *do* any of this stuff until I met Lisa. My family wasn't into their cultural roots. You know my dad, he kind of got away from all that when he moved off the reservation in northern Idaho, met Mom, and moved to Jasper," Thomas shrugged.

"That's okay," Logan said, "My grandmother tried to wipe out all traces of our Appalachian roots. Told us we were descended from a Scottish earl. Wanted to skip the dirt-poor, mountain people part of our history."

She turned to Lisa, "What dance are you going to be doing, again?"

"I won't be doing any dance if we don't get moving," Lisa said, scooting out of the booth. "And neither will Mrs. White-horse if I don't get that jingle dress to her."

They paid the bill and piled into the van.

"When we get to the powwow, they'll have a program that will list all the main dances and stuff. We'll get you one and Thomas can explain as they go."

26

Lisa chatted happily with Logan while Thomas kept an eye out for the turnoff. In spite of morning traffic, it only took them ten minutes. The Oakdale powwow, like many others, was held on the county fairgrounds. They parked by one of the side entrances, and were able to carry everything in one load. Lisa had one of those carts on wheels, and Thomas carried Mrs. Whitehorse's dress, which Lisa said weighed over ten pounds, over his arm.

When they entered the gate, there was an information table with a few t-shirts and bumper stickers for sale. Logan picked up a program and began thumbing through it while Lisa went to deliver the jingle dress. When Logan had asked her about the silver cones on the dress, Lisa had explained that, like people everywhere, Native Americans in the eighteen hundreds were innovative recyclers, using whatever materials were at hand. The original jingles were made from the metal lids of snuff cans that had been left lying around by the soldiers. They curled them into individual cones, punched a hole at the top, and sewed it onto the dress in rows. The metal cones made a soft jingling sound when the woman danced, thus the name.

Thomas went to get, unbelievably, a snack. He came back with a couple of churros, long twists of cinnamon-sugar donuts, and a Coke. "We're in luck, the stands aren't busy yet. It's still early."

He offered Logan one, which she accepted—cinnamon-sugar being an important food group as far as she was concerned. The program had short explanations for each dance, but Thomas warned her "Don't put too much stock in that. There are a lot of different Indian stories out there for where each dance comes from."

By then, Lisa had returned and all three set off to explore the craft booths. The Grand Entry was scheduled to begin just after noon.

Logan checked her watch. It was 9:50 a.m. so they had plenty of time to wander around, one of Logan's favorite things to do. For the next two hours, she immersed herself in the sights, smells, and sounds of the powwow. There was a lot to see.

A tall man walked by, black and white feathers fanned out from his painted face and arms. What little clothing he wore looked like it was made of beautiful, butter-soft buckskin. But the amazing part was that he was as blonde as Ben and had more freckles than Logan. No one batted an eye as he strolled through the crowd.

In one of the booths they passed, a group of three women in brightly colored outfits were combing through bins of colorful beads, making their selections. Logan was surprised to see neon green and pink fringe on one woman's dress. She'd expected everything native to be natural like the buckskin guy.

Lisa saw her looking and said, "Yeah, people expect all Indians to look like they did in the eighteenth century, but we're a living, changing culture. We have a lot of disagreements among ourselves as to what is traditional and what isn't."

SHATTERED

Many of the older men wore jeans and long-sleeved western shirts and hats, looking more like cowboys than Indians. She also saw quite a few men of all ages in military uniforms, fatigues mostly. Logan wondered what that was about.

Every five feet or so, they were stopped by someone Lisa knew. When Lisa asked after a mutual friend, an older woman gestured with her bottom lip in the direction of another booth.

"It is impolite to point with your finger," Lisa explained as they walked over to the indicated booth. "She is *Diné*, Navajo."

Logan had just about reached cultural overload and was beginning to feel hunger pangs when they bumped into Thomas, and Lisa suggested a rest and lunch.

Wonderful smells engulfed them as they passed taco, tamale, and hot dog stands, but Thomas made a beeline for the last stall in the back of the row.

"Longest line, but worth the wait!" Lisa said.

The wait was indeed worth it. The fry bread was as awesome as advertised. Logan had hers with powdered sugar and a bowl of *posole*, a Mexican soup made with pork and white corn she always got at Juan's whenever it was available, which was usually during the holidays.

An hour later, bellies full, they made their way over to the dance grounds. There was still some space in the bleachers. After delivering Mrs. Whitehorse's dress, Lisa went to the bathroom to change into her outfit.

Logan enjoyed watching the children running excitedly up and down the aisles and the women helping each other make last minute adjustments to their hair or accessories. Thomas looked at his phone, frowned, and said he'd be right back.

When Lisa returned, she was wearing what she said was a northern style women's traditional dress, which included knee-length beaded moccasins, and a long, buckskin dress with open sleeves, on which she had completely beaded the shoulder area.

She carried a fringed shawl over her left arm, a purse, and a feather fan, made of eagle feathers which, Logan knew from Thomas, were illegal for anyone but Native Americans to possess. Lisa's whole demeanor and way of moving had changed since she had donned her dancing outfit. She looked positively regal.

Logan's friend stood taller, spoke slower, and her movements took on a more dignified, graceful manner. As she made her way to the edge of the arena with the other women dancing northern traditional, she seemed to glide effortlessly across the ground.

At about 12:30 p.m., the Grand Entry got started. The drummers sat in a circle at the edge of the field and began a steady beat, singing words Logan did not understand, leading in the dancers, who formed a loose line.

Just when she started to worry Thomas wouldn't get back in time, he appeared at her side. He didn't explain where he'd gone, but it was probably business. She was so glad she wasn't tied to a phone anymore. Clients could be so demanding. At least teaching didn't come with a pager. Before thoughts of her tenuous job situation could intrude, Logan firmly pushed them in the back of her mind. Today was about having fun, learning new things, and watching Lisa dance.

"What are the guys in uniform for?" Logan asked. "I saw a lot of them today."

"Those are the veterans." Thomas said. "They're honored at every powwow. They are considered to have strong medicine because they survived war. Then come the elders of the tribes, the men dancers, then the women dancers . . . There's Lisa . . . and then the kids are last."

SHATTERED

The hours floated together, and after several more dances, lots of visiting, and an honor dance for a woman whose son had just graduated from UCSD, they made their way back to the motel.

Logan planned on sleeping in. Her visiting quota was more than filled. She needed some alone time.

Under Lisa's guidance, she had purchased an instructional drum DVD she thought might be fun to combine with the African *djembe*, a large drum she had brought to school for the kids last year. She had been thinking of ways to tie music in with the math and social studies curriculum.

The three friends said their good nights and, after receiving another one of Lisa's care packages, she gratefully closed the door on a fun, but very long day. Selecting a Heath bar from the bag, she unwrapped it and took a bite while pulling off her jeans and boots.

She took a second bite and then a third, polishing it off before taking a hot shower. Rummaging in her overnight bag, she pulled out a pair of pale blue cotton pajama bottoms and a cami that Amy had gotten her for her birthday last year.

Too tired to floss, she swirled some water around in a half-hearted attempt at getting the rest of the toffee from the Heath bar unstuck from one of her back molars. Yawning deeply, she crawled into bed, body tired and mind full. She began reading the slim book that came with the powwow drum DVD, but it wasn't even 10:30 p.m. before the remote slipped from her hand. In the mysterious language of dreams, the drum, the heartbeat of the powwow, became her pulse.

27

The back gate now locked behind the last policeman, Iona retired her No. 2 pencil, checked her bag for cigarettes and lighter, popped her gum, and hurried toward her car for a much-anticipated rendezvous with one of her favorite male friends, Bernie, a long-haul truck driver just in from Idaho, down at Mullies.

Murder or no murder, she'd put in a full day. Someone had to help those idiot cops. Not a brain cell between them. They'd had a week since that poor girl was discovered, and they hadn't done diddlysquat as far as she could see. No one was allowed back in yet to the glassblowing area, but Detective Andrews said maybe Monday.

Iona glowered at a knot of neon yellow police tape still attached to one section of the fence, littering her grounds, and muttered another choice expletive. She'd have to have one of the guys go through and make sure all that was off before Monday, should Mr. High-and-Mighty Police Detective

Andrews decide to release them from limbo. She would have done it herself, but she was late already.

Licking her index finger, she wiped a smudge of mascara off her bottom eyelid, while looking in the rear-view mirror, illuminated only by the harsh yellow light of the parking lot. Her interior light was out.

"Damn raccoon eyes," she muttered.

Makeup fixed and peppermint lifesaver popped in her mouth, she turned the key in her Barracuda fastback, threw it into reverse, and began backing out. Over the sounds of crunching gravel she heard someone yelling at her.

Peering out the driver's side window, she saw one of her new puppy guards—she swore they got younger and younger every year—standing behind the gate, waving her down with one hand, proudly holding a very unhappy and bewildered young man by the scruff of the neck with the other.

Iona sighed, swore, and shifted into first. Bernie would have to wait.

Before she got the gate unlocked, the guard chirped excitedly, "Caught him hiding out in the dumpster! Guess the police didn't think to look in there today."

Ignoring the guard's boastful chatter, she leaned over to the young captive and whispered in his ear, "I'm so sorry, Danny. Tell your Mom I tried to help."

She had no choice. The police were called, and within the hour, Danny Schultz, Neva's runaway son, back from Portland, OR, was taken into custody as a suspect in the murder of Catherine Elizabeth Woods.

*****

SHATTERED

He liked the rain. It was soft and made everything green, so much greener than Southern California, where he came from. He liked it more when he was looking at it from inside a nice, warm house, though. It sure rained a lot here.

Just a few weeks ago they'd been living with James' friend out in the studio over the garage his parents had fixed up for him so he could practice his music away from the house. It was warm. The woman had even let him come into the house and help her make bread once. It reminded him of his Mom. He liked to help her in the kitchen too, he loved the smell of things baking in the oven, and he didn't even mind doing the dishes. He washed each one carefully and his mom always said he did a great job. But his dad didn't like it, said he didn't understand why he wanted to do women's work.

Then James and Mark got into a fight, and they had to move to a hotel. James was really smart and told Danny not to worry. Even though it hadn't worked out at the hotel, James found them this place, where they could stay for free. It wasn't as nice, but he said it was temporary.

No water came out of the faucets and the lights didn't work, but there was a place to go to the bathroom. You just had to follow the Xs James had marked on the doors for them, until you got to the other side of the building. The only problem was you couldn't flush or wash your hands like his mother had taught him to do. You could sit down, but it wasn't very warm.

When they left California for their Oregon adventure, James said he knew a drummer in a band up in Portland. You didn't have to know much to bang on stuff and shake some bells, James told him. He could pick that up in a few weeks and BAM! They'd have money and a great vacation! He said he'd have them home in no time, with money in their pocket in just a few weeks.

James looked a little funny when he came in this morning, all sort of fidgety. He said he'd been out all night making them some money. He had a bag with two egg McMuffins, one of those hash brown patties, which wasn't crunchy anymore, but that was okay. He gave it all to Danny, then sat looking out the window, hugging his knees. He said he didn't want any.

It felt so good to be full, and Danny slept, even though the floor was hard and not very clean.

When he woke up, James was waiting for him, walking back and forth, looking serious.

"We're going out, Danny. I need you to do what I say, okay?"

"Sure, James."

"We're just going to go down to this little store a ways down the street."

When Danny still looked blank, James added, "You know, Mr. Kim's place where I got you those Slim Jims? All you need to do is go shopping, Danny. Just pick out a few things you'd like to eat. Get at least three things. And take your time. I'll show you where to look. There are some good things in the back of the store."

"Okay. I'm not that hungry, now, James. That McDonald's was good. I'm all full, really. You don't have to buy me anything until you get a job. I can get a job, too, James." He was worried that James was getting so skinny.

"Yeah, I know you can, Danny. But just do this for me now, okay? Don't look at me when we go in, but listen. I'll tell you when we're done shopping. Just do as I say."

"Okay. Whatever you say, James."

"Now get your coat on. We're moving. By tonight we'll have a warm place with beds."

28

Still half asleep, Logan shook her head, trying to locate the source of the jarring and persistent ringing. She squinted at the fluorescent dial of the motel clock on the nightstand. Why she thought knowing the time of day would help, she didn't know. It's just what people did when they were disoriented.

The blinding light streaming in under the curtains didn't help, but she finally identified the guilty party, her cell phone. She rubbed her eyes and cleared her throat, tapped the screen, and put it on speaker.

"Hello" she said, trying to sound more awake than she felt.

"Logan?"

"Yeah. Rick?"

"Yeah, it's me. I'm not calling from my cell—glad you picked up. Just wanted to let you know they're going to reopen the festival for sure. Probably Monday. They have a suspect in custody for that girl's murder."

"Oh," she felt guilty for having pushed the murder to the back of her mind, "that was fast," Logan responded. "Who did they arrest?"

"Remember Danny, Neva's kid?"

"Danny? You're kidding. I didn't even know he was still around."

"No one else did either. He was hiding out in the festival. Pretty successfully, too. His Mom helped him. He stayed in her booth at night. Next morning he'd leave when the crowds got thick enough. So many kids with hoodies, he just blended in. She left food for him. Don't know where he went during the day. They found him last night. I just heard about it."

"Who was he hiding from?"

"The police up in Portland. He's wanted in a robbery up there, liquor store."

"Danny? He was slow, but he was a good kid as far as I know. Never got into any trouble here. And how did he even get to Portland? Could he drive a car? And why would he want to kill Elizabeth? When did he get back?"

"Don't know. His friend, the guy they caught, had drugs on him. Who knows how Danny may have changed if he was into drugs. He's not a little kid anymore. Anyway, people do things you'd never think they'd do when drugs are involved. Andrews will figure it out. Just let Thomas and Lisa know about the festival, would you? Iona will let you guys know for sure, but I think they've given the okay and it'll be open tomorrow."

"Of course, I'll tell them. We're heading back today. Are you off tonight?"

"Should be."

"You and Charlie want to come over for dinner?"

"Ben's cooking and Thomas and Lisa are coming," she added.

"We'll be there if we don't get called in," Rick said.

Logan breathed a sigh of relief that at least Thomas was not being looked at by the police, although she still wondered why he'd been at the festival that morning. Had he seen Danny? And if so, why hadn't he said anything? Too many unanswered questions. But, she reminded herself, she didn't have to answer any of them tonight. She was just going to enjoy her friends.

Lisa had everything packed the night before, so after a shower and breakfast, at which Logan wisely avoided the fruit cup, they were on the road before 10:00 a.m. Even with an overturned truck on Highway 91 outside of Norco, costing them an extra thirty-minute slowdown, Thomas got them home by noon. That left Logan plenty of time to check in with Ben to see about dinner. Mr. Prepared had all the food ready, so all she had to do was make sure the guest bathroom was clean and help set the picnic table. It was a great night.

Ben and Thomas hit it off immediately. Maybe it was their mutual love of the natural world. Thomas had some pictures of his work on his phone and Ben gave him a tour of the garden. Everyone liked Ben, even Rick, although Logan knew Ben was still under "cop/brother" scrutiny, and probably always would be. Rick had never liked Jack.

An unfamiliar sense of happiness welled up within her. When Bonnie and Mike came back from their vacation, they'd all have to get together. Maybe life could be normal again, or better than normal. If there was one thing the last two years had taught her, it was that you never knew what life held in store.

29

There was a loud banging on the door. Thomas told Lisa to stay in bed. He'd go see who it was. With a growing sense of dread, he padded down the hall and looked out the peephole in the front door.

Two men in suits filled the fisheye view. A police car could be seen behind them, parked at the end of the driveway. Not wanting to, but knowing he had no choice, Thomas opened the door, trying to look like having two cops show up on his doorstep at 5:00 a.m. on a Monday morning was normal.

Unfortunately, he recognized them.

"Thomas Delgado?" The man on the left asked, as if he wasn't sure who Thomas was, even though he'd just questioned Thomas down at the station less than a week ago.

No, I'm Mickey Mouse.

Thomas' mind rapidly spiraled through any way he could stop this. Any way he could protect Lisa. The only question was how much these guys knew.

The man didn't identify himself, but Thomas remembered his name. Detective Andrews. The other one was Diaz, also a detective.

"We need you to come down to the station with us. We'd like to ask you a few more questions about your relationship with the deceased, Elizabeth Catherine Woods."

"Shouldn't you be reading him his rights?" Lisa demanded, coming up behind Thomas, wrapping a thin robe around her. She stood as tall as she could next to her husband, violet eyes flashing.

"No, ma'am, your husband is not under arrest. We'd just like to talk with him," Andrews said.

The other detective remained silent.

"Can't you talk with him here?" she asked, stepping aside to let them in, somewhat mollified by the fact that no one was clapping handcuffs on her husband.

"Not really," Andrews said, "This might take a while."

She started to say something more, but Thomas cut her off.

"It's okay," he said. "No problem, Detective. I'll come down with you. Just let me put on some clothes."

He gave Lisa a small hug and turned back toward the bedroom.

"Sure," Andrews said.

They had an officer on the back door. The guy wasn't going anywhere but back to the station.

30

At barely five pounds, Elizabeth Catherine Glover seemed too fragile for her weighty, royal names. An avid historical romance fan, her mother had christened her baby after England's Queen Elizabeth and Catherine the Great of Russia.

But the tiny towhead survived her premature birth and soon was released from the hospital to go home. The first eleven years of her life were blissfully uneventful.

Two days before her twelfth birthday, her father died of a massive heart attack no one saw coming. He'd been young and healthy and there had been no history of heart disease on either side of his family. Her mother, never strong to begin with, retreated into a depressed half-life for several years. Elizabeth was left alone to mourn them both. She didn't have much time for self-pity, though. There was school, there was work, and eventually, there was Frank.

Due to the life insurance, Elizabeth and her mom were okay financially, if they were careful with their spending, which

Elizabeth was. She took over the running of the household when it was obvious her mother couldn't handle it.

The two of them settled into a routine. Elizabeth learned to make dinner and mow the lawn. Mr. Larson even taught her to change the spark plugs on the Buick. She made sure her mother took her 'nerve pills' on her bad nights, so she could sleep. And with all this, she kept her grades up. Not because her mother ever checked, but because school wasn't that hard. She was light years ahead of the other kids in math. She did her assignments religiously, out of habit, even though no one checked her homework anymore.

Eventually, her mother left the house, venturing as far as one of the neighbors' back yards for dinner and a blind date the neighbor had arranged. Elizabeth was so young, she thought a blind date meant the man couldn't see.

But he could see all right, and what he saw was her mother, looking cool and radiant that night, legs crossed lazily, head tilted, her soft, Southern features glowing in the fire light, listening raptly to Frank go on about something.

Within a year, much to Elizabeth's disgust, they were married. For a while, it was okay. But when she sprouted breasts, Frank's attentions turned from her mother to her, wanting her to sit closer to him on the couch. The already awkward living situation became impossible. She got an after-school job and started wearing baggy clothes.

Her new job was at a local glassblowers' studio, cleaning and doing the setup, in addition to babysitting a neighbor's two kids. The woman worked swing shift on the weekends, which suited Elizabeth just fine. It provided Frank with a plausible excuse for her longer absences from the house.

Focused on her future, she went on very few dates. By the time she reached her senior year of high school she'd been dubbed 'Elizabeth the Ice Queen' by the boys she wouldn't put out for and something worse by the girls in town who did.

Her Dad had started a college fund for her, but Frank had gone through most of it already. There was to be no college. She'd have to finance her own escape.

The glassblower, a sixty-two-year-old named Bob Wilson, seeing her interest in his work, eventually let her assist him from time to time. He said the young girl was a natural—quiet and not boy crazy like other girls her age. He'd always had male assistants in the shop, but Elizabeth proved to be strong and more reliable than her male predecessors. She showed up, worked hard, and didn't chew gum.

When she broke a piece she'd labored over, she didn't whine, cuss or kick things, but asked what she did wrong and started over. Once she cried, but she got over it. He'd never seen anyone so focused or intent on becoming the best.

Within a year, he entered her in a local glassblowing competition. It was the week after graduation. Delighted with her victory, she slipped into bed and put her winning piece on her nightstand, planning to show it to Mr. Wilson the next day. She couldn't wait to share her victory with her mentor in the morning. She'd gotten in the habit of joining him and his wife for breakfast Sunday mornings before the shop opened.

Wilson had an idea things weren't right at home for his young assistant for a while now, and his concern was validated when she showed up with a black eye and some bruises on her arm instead of the excited smile he was expecting after he heard of her win.

Frank had not been impressed with her trophy. He knocked her down, threw her prize against the wall, and then made her clean it up and throw the pieces away in the trash. Elizabeth didn't tell her boss this, of course, but it wasn't too tough to figure out she didn't get that black eye by bumping into a door.

Bob made a decision. The girl was almost nineteen. He beefed up her next paycheck with enough to get her across country on a Grayhound to his friend, Howard Miller, out in California. Bob knew he'd taken on a few interns in the last couple of years, starting a sort of school out there, and she'd be in good hands. Howard was a good man. The girl was talented and a hard worker. She'd do okay.

"Poor kid," he confided to his wife when he got home that night, "Hope she'll be all right."

"At least she'll be safe with Howard," her wife replied, patting his hand reassuringly.

31

Iona's group message last night said the festival would reopen in the morning, so Logan went in at her regularly scheduled time, only to find no one at the booth. She walked around back to make sure Thomas and Lisa weren't just late setting up, but no one was there. She pulled out her cell and called their house.

"Lisa? This is Logan. Where are you guys? I'm down here at the festival . . . you're not."

Uncharacteristic silence was all she heard. Finally, Lisa spoke, but she could hardly hear her.

"It's all my fault, Logan. They've taken Thomas back down to the police station and this time it's serious. This whole mess is *my fault!*" She started crying after that, and Logan could get nothing more out of her.

"Don't move. I'll be right there. Everything's going to be okay."

Things were definitely not okay, and she had no idea how she could help, but Logan was on the road again in less than five minutes. On the way, she called Rick.

When he picked up, she blurted, "Lisa said they just picked up Thomas again. I thought they already had a suspect, Danny, in custody? Why'd they pull Thomas in again? What is going on?"

"I don't know. First I heard. Call you right back."

Five minutes later, her cell phone rang. She was still in her car, so she tapped her Bluetooth to answer.

"I talked to Keith, a friend of mine in the coroner's office. He said they'd kick Danny except for the Portland charge, but they don't think it's related. Thomas is who they're really interested in. The Orange County ME found an obsidian knife tip embedded underneath one of Elizabeth's ribs. Since Thomas is the only one who deals with obsidian at the festival, they want to talk to him. They've been doing a lot of digging. Got warrants. They didn't find a knife when they searched the cage, though, or Thomas and Lisa's booth. Just the regular ones in the case he made. So far, they still have no murder weapon."

"There must be more to it. They can't just arrest him because he makes obsidian knives. I just talked to Lisa and she's really upset."

"There is. Given that this is a murder case, Keith said the judge gave a pretty wide search warrant. While searching his booth, they found a note in Thomas's calendar for a substantial withdrawal six weeks ago. They're subpoenaing the bank records now. They'll hold him until they can untangle all this.

"Couldn't he have been buying supplies or paying a bill, or starting a 401K? Why didn't they just ask him what it was for? He could have answered that over the phone instead of hauling him into the station. Lisa's a wreck. I'm on my way there now."

"They didn't have to. They already have Elizabeth's bank records. The same amount was deposited into Elizabeth

Woods' bank account the next day. Thomas lied. He told them he barely knew her. It doesn't look good."

Rick took in a deep breath while this news sank in.

"I know you're upset, Logan, but I'm sure if Thomas is innocent, this will all get straightened out," Rick said.

If Thomas was innocent? Did Rick doubt him?

He didn't know Thomas as well as she did. Rick was a few years behind them in school. He'd never sat with Thomas behind the bleachers and talked and seen him rescue an injured baby bird and nurse it back to life, feeding it through an eye-dropper twenty-four seven. He didn't know Thomas. She did.

It looked bad, but there had to be an explanation. Logan searched her brain. Maybe Thomas loaned Elizabeth the money. Then why did he say he barely knew her? The fact that Thomas had lied to her was almost more unbelievable than that he was capable of doing something violent. Given enough provocation, anyone was capable of violence.

"And Logan, there's one more thing."

What more could there possibly be?

"According to the ME, Elizabeth was five weeks pregnant."

With that news, there didn't seem to be much else to say, although she knew there must be a logical explanation. Hopefully, Lisa would have one, since she couldn't exactly call Thomas right now and ask him.

After making Rick promise to call her as soon as he heard anything more, she added, almost as an afterthought before they were disconnected, "Keep me posted about Danny."

She let Rick and Charlie get back to work and drove to Thomas and Lisa's place. She got out of her car and crossed the yard in a few long strides. Lisa opened the door before she could knock.

Somewhat more composed by the time Logan arrived, Lisa was still a shadow of the strong, radiant woman who had proudly danced with such confidence and poise at the powwow. Her skin was a gray mask, eyes rimmed red, but her hand was steady when she set a mug of strong, black coffee in front of Logan, motioning for her to sit as she lowered herself heavily onto the couch, curling her feet under her. She looked exhausted.

Clenching and unclenching her hands, Lisa said, "None of this makes any sense without you knowing the whole story. Thomas trusts you, but I know he's too stubborn and too protective of me to tell anyone, even you, why he gave Elizabeth that money."

Logan wasn't sure she wanted to hear this, but friendship trumped doubt.

"Thomas was always there for me, Lisa, even when my Mom left. He was my rock. No matter what you have to tell me, none of that changes. I'm here for him. And for you, too," Logan assured her.

32

Lisa let out a ragged breath. She looked down at her hands, twisting the tissue between her fingers, then back up at Logan.

"They arrested Thomas. He is in jail because he is protecting me."

"You?" Logan asked, "What'd you do, rob a bank when moccasins weren't selling?"

Lisa managed a weary smile.

"When I was in college, I was different. I didn't know Thomas then, we met later . . . after."

She was getting the words out with difficulty. "I was angry back then . . . for a lot of reasons."

Logan waited for her to continue, still not seeing how this applied to Thomas, or Elizabeth's murder.

"We thought—well, the people I hung out with then thought we could change things. I started dating an older guy, a Native American activist on campus named George Hawkings.

"He was a good talker, good looking, and very intense. And I was ripe for the attention. I know you probably won't understand this, but he made me feel fully Indian, fully Native.

Living on the reservation, I sometimes didn't fit in. You know," she gestured with a circular motion to her face, "these eyes, my skin. My nickname was Paleface.

"I think that made me want to prove my 'Indianness' all the more. George educated me, I'll give him that. First, about sex, I was so young, then about water rights, fishing rights, land rights. So many things were stolen from us—and not just a long time ago, he said. It was still happening!"

Lisa sat up, and her tone became more strident. There was a fire in her eyes Logan had never seen before.

"Before I met George, I thought the bad things that had happened, the injustices, were all in the past: small pox on the trade blankets, the Trail of Tears, but I didn't know they were still trying to take things from us. It was an ongoing battle, and later, in George's mind, an ongoing war."

She continued, "George was pre-law, very intelligent, a natural leader. He called the group of us *The Way*. It was peaceful at first, just a bunch of kids—some white, mostly Indian—getting together in the student union or wherever, learning about the past, taking pride in our heritage. But then it changed.

"George said once you knew about something, you were obligated to do something about it, so we wrote letters, we marched. But nothing happened. Nothing we were doing did any good. People thought we were nuts dredging up old history. Why didn't we just leave the past in the past, leave well enough alone? Blah, blah, blah. We heard a lot of that. In hindsight, I can see that George directed our anger and used it.

"It started with a water rights issue. The government wanted to take even more water away from George's already struggling tribe, to give it to a big agricultural interest in the state.

Oklahoma's big in soybeans and cotton, both thirsty crops. Their lobbyists bought off the senators. It was just a matter of time.

"We tried to get anyone at the newspaper or local TV station to interview George or write an article, but nobody was listening to a bunch of kids, particularly not a bunch of rez Indian kids. It wasn't cool back then to be Indian.

"George got really frustrated. Finally, he convinced us that we had to do something dramatic to get some attention, before any more tribal members sold their land, or their water rights if they'd managed to hang onto their land, scattering the community even farther apart.

"He said if we could take over the local Bureau of Indian Affairs office, they'd have to listen to us. If he could get it in the papers, people would see how unfair it was and leave what little water there was with the people who needed it. He wasn't even trying to gain ground, just keep any more from being taken.

"The local Indian agent's name was William DeBrea, and he fought George every step of the way. George, going by the name "One Knife" by then, decided to make a statement by lighting up DeBrea's office one night after work."

Lisa looked up, begging Logan to understand with her eyes, "None of us knew what he was going to do. Later, George told us he hadn't planned on anyone being there, but the Indian agent, DeBrea, was working late that night, preparing for a hearing in the morning. He made it out of the building, but was badly burned.

"George called the papers and took credit for the incident. He gave credit to *all* of us in the group; but we didn't know anything about it! He'd gone off the deep end. He and I had been having trouble before that—and that was the last straw.

"But I was connected, even though I didn't know what he was planning or doing that night. Everyone knew I was George's girlfriend. We'd been living together until a few months before. I wasn't with him when he did it. I didn't know, but I didn't think anyone would believe me, so I ran.

"I was twenty-one years old and didn't know what else to do. None of us did. Everyone scattered, went underground.

"The FBI got him, eventually. I think after that they stopped looking for the rest of us. They must have figured out it was a one-man job, but we were never exonerated. It's not like I can go to the nearest FBI office and ask, "Oh, by the way, am I still wanted?" Lisa looked up with a wry half smile, and just as quickly went back to examining her hands.

Lisa took a deep breath and composed herself, "I would have turned myself in then, but I had a three-month old baby and I could not support her if I was in prison."

33

This was shocking news. Logan never knew Lisa had a child. She felt a rush of sympathy for the young, scared mother Lisa must have been. Here she'd known her for years and had been working with the woman all summer, but didn't know something this important. It made her wonder if any of us know each other very well.

She couldn't imagine giving Amy up, under any circumstances, but she could not judge Lisa. Life had a lot more gray areas than most people were comfortable with. No one knows what he or she would do for sure, until faced with the decision.

"Where did you go? How did you manage?" Logan asked.

"I changed my name. I worked. I sent money back to my mother, who raised her. I wound up losing her anyway to meningitis two years later. I couldn't even go to her funeral. I haven't seen my mother in over fifteen years."

Logan thought Lisa was going to collapse from the weight of these dredged up memories, but she straightened her shoulders. She ended her story quietly, placing the red beads, finally, in the bowl.

"Mr. DeBrea died in the ER."

No wonder she ran.

"I am so sorry, Lisa. All of that can't be easy to have carried around all these years, but you do know that you are not responsible for that man's death."

Lisa did not look reassured.

"You didn't know what he was planning, and you wouldn't have had any part of it if you had."

"But I couldn't prove that. And I had followed George, we all had. Maybe he wouldn't have acted if we hadn't fed his ego."

Lisa's eyes began filling with tears, "Maybe I'm not directly responsible, but I should have left George sooner, when I saw the direction he was going. We all got swept up in his vision. We believed him. I should have seen it coming. He was so angry all the time. It helped me put my own anger in perspective. I should have told someone . . . or done something . . ." Lisa looked very small, curled up in the corner of the couch.

After waiting a few minutes, she took a deep breath and continued, "After my daughter died, I moved to New Mexico. That's where I met Thomas."

When Lisa mentioned Thomas' name, Logan noticed her shoulders relax and her face light up.

"Thomas accepted my past, helped me accept things I could not change. He even admired the part of me that wanted to change the world. He taught me to focus on the here and now, on more productive ways to do good."

Lisa completely shredded the tissue, balled it up and placed it in the ashtray on the coffee table. Thomas still smoked.

Both women sat quietly while Logan digested this new information and contemplated where things stood.

Now at least she understood why Thomas hadn't wanted the police to start asking questions and unearth Lisa's past.

Logan felt completely out of her element. She knew nothing about the FBI or statutes of limitations, proof of innocence, or anything about how she could help her friends, but at least she knew now what she was dealing with, and that always felt better than being in the dark.

Getting back to the original reason for the story, Thomas being blackmailed, "So, why did Thomas give Elizabeth $8,000? Had she found out about all this somehow?"

"She overheard a phone call. Thought Thomas was paying to cover something up *he* had done. Something mundane, like having an affair. I wish it were something so boring.

"Elizabeth misunderstood the conversation, and Thomas decided it would be better to let her think badly of him and pay her than to risk my past coming out before we had a chance to clear it up. The man he was talking to was a private investigator, ex-FBI. With his connections, he was doing some digging to see if they were still looking for me, or ever had been. If they were, he was looking into helping me clear my name."

"Why now? I mean . . . you've been living with this for a long time. What made you want to dig into all of this now? You have a new life, a new name."

"Fair question. About a year ago, I was diagnosed with lupus, that's why I'm tired a lot, and it's getting worse. I have good days and bad days. Lupus is categorized as an autoimmune disease by western medicine, but according to my aunt, who is a healer, disease means you are out of harmony and balance with the natural world. When I was going through a really bad flare-up with the lupus this winter, I spent some time with her. I realized I needed to clean out my past, to make amends as much as possible, to bring myself back in balance, before attempting a healing ceremony for the lupus, which she wants to do for me."

Lisa looked up at Logan's face, "I know this all must sound silly to you."

Logan didn't have an opinion one way or the other about Native American beliefs about healing or sickness, but reassured Lisa she did not think she was silly for wanting to set things straight.

"How was all of this supposed to work?" Logan asked.

34

"We hired an attorney as well as the private investigator. Thomas has been taking extra jobs for collectors, making replicas, to pay for all this. We asked the investigator to first find any remaining relatives of Mr. DeBrea, so I could make whatever amends I could.

"Turns out Mr. DeBrea had one child, a daughter, who is in her junior year of high school now. She's a good student, but her Mom is not well off. We were so happy, because at last there was something concrete I could do to right the wrongs of the past. We decided to find a way to help her go to college. Anonymously, of course, we'd set up a scholarship. She'd probably never accept it otherwise.

"The attorney said that we could set it up to look like a scholarship program she won. She has good grades. It doesn't make up for her being raised without a father, but it's something I can do. She more than deserves it."

Logan couldn't help but think of how much Lisa must miss her own little girl, who never got to grow up, let alone go to college. Helping this girl would help Lisa honor her own daughter's memory. She wondered if Lisa saw the connection.

"All that was left was for the private investigator to find evidence that proved I had nothing to do with the firebombing or that man's death. We've been waiting to hear from him. He could clear Thomas easily, but Thomas won't let me call him."

Lisa took a deep breath.

"So that's why Thomas isn't talking to the police," she said, "he has an alibi that explains why he let Elizabeth blackmail him even though he wasn't guilty of anything. He only wants to protect me, so he won't tell the police the truth. He wasn't worried about her coming back for more money, because everything will be out in the open as soon as the investigator gets back to us. That or I'll be arrested. Either way, Thomas had no motive to hurt Elizabeth. And of course, he would never harm anyone."

"Of course," Logan said.

Logan didn't think that Lisa confessing would help Thomas. They would just think he murdered Elizabeth to stop additional blackmail. And in the back of her mind was the nagging question. Who was the father of Elizabeth's baby?

"Thomas is protecting me, but I can't keep letting him do that. Whether or not we hear my name is cleared with the FBI yet, I'm going to the police."

"Sounds like the best way to help you and get Thomas off the suspect list is to find out who really killed Elizabeth Woods. That way no one will dig around in your past, and you can do whatever you need to feel at peace," said Logan.

That was the best outcome any of them could hope for, but way above her pay grade.

Lisa's violet eyes flashed with new strength, "I already called and asked to see Detective Andrews as soon as possible. They said he'd probably be in after 9:00 a.m. I'm supposed to call then and make an appointment. I'm going in there in person to talk to him. I'm not leaving there without Thomas."

Logan discouraged her from taking any action yet reminding her that Thomas had explicitly insisted she wait until Friday.

"I told the investigator last night that he had to let me know one way or the other by Friday," Lisa said. "I'm not waiting any longer than that. I only promised Thomas I'd wait until then."

Lisa abruptly stood and began pacing.

"I want Thomas out of there," she said. "If the investigator hasn't found out anything by then, I'm going in to talk with Detective Andrews, no matter *what* Thomas says!"

"I understand how you feel, Lisa, but hang in there. Thomas is a big boy, you couldn't change his mind if you wanted to anyway. You know how stubborn he is," Logan admonished in as comforting a tone as she could muster.

She tried to get Lisa's mind on something other than going down to the police station, "What made the investigator think he may have good news for you?"

"He didn't want to get my hopes up, he said, so wasn't more specific. It's been so long, I'm afraid to hope, but whatever the news is, I'm ready to face it. It's time, and it's what I need to do to get well."

"Don't go turning yourself in, yet, Lisa. Wait, okay? Rick says he's okay where he's at. He's safe. I know that's what Thomas wants you to do. If it's good news, great. If not, you can always turn yourself in then," she said, hoping it would never come to that. The thought of Lisa in jail was not something she wanted to contemplate.

Lisa promised, but Logan wasn't completely convinced. There was that certain something in her voice. She realized if she was going to keep Lisa from marching in to turn herself in to Detective Andrews for crimes she hadn't committed, that had occurred over sixteen years ago, she, Logan, would have to figure out who the real murderer was. She couldn't trust the federal government to not throw Lisa in jail, just to check a box and close a file.

The only way to get Thomas released, and keep Lisa's past private, was to find the true killer. The only trouble was, she had no idea where to start. Relieved at having unburdened herself to a friend, but emotionally and physically exhausted, Lisa went to lay down and Logan got on the road.

As she drove home, Logan reviewed their conversation. Thomas was acting out of a sense of loyalty, which was admirable. In the meantime, there was a dead girl cooling her heels in the morgue. Someone had brutally murdered her. Someone the police weren't even looking for as long as Thomas was suspect number one.

35

Logan felt anything but the confident, capable friend she'd portrayed to Lisa when they talked earlier. With nothing planned for the rest of the day, she grabbed a fork and spoon from one of the kitchen drawers and went out to attack the weeds in the yard. She'd have to add yard implements to her growing list of homeowner supplies to buy. A couple hours later, she slapped together a sandwich and called it dinner. She fed Dimebox, wiped down the kitchen counters and, with nothing else to do, plopped down on the couch. She didn't even feel like playing Bella.

She was absolutely wiped out, but it was too early to go to bed. She wondered how Lisa was holding up. Even if Thomas could be cleared, Lisa might be next. Although it was preposterous, Detective Andrews, once he knew about Lisa's past, might assume if she was involved with violence once, she could be violent again. People killed for less, a lot less, according to the nightly news. And what if the baby was Thomas's? She didn't even want to think about that.

Although minor in comparison, Logan was reminded of some very real problems in her own life she would need to deal with soon. First, she was as good as fired, according to the letter she'd received on the last day of school, and second, that damned pink shoebox was still at the bottom of her closet. Then there was the rest of her personal life, or lack thereof.

Ben had been pretty much MIA since the BBQ. She'd sent him on his way again last night without inviting him to stay over. Why couldn't she get rid of these archaic ideas about sex? Why was she holding out? Did any of the rules she had gone by so strictly growing up even matter anymore? And she hadn't heard from Bonnie in a while or had an email from Amy in over a week. Had she pissed everyone off? Let someone down? How could she be expected to focus with everything else going on? God, she sucked at relationships.

She stomped into the kitchen and looked glumly at her wine selection. She was down to one bottle of chardonnay Rick gave her as a housewarming gift, but chose to abstain. Too many Phoenix burgers and Ben's food offerings in the past couple of weeks had made her pants harder to zip than usual. If this kept up, she'd have to start shopping for mom jeans, or just go directly to sweats or XL yoga pants.

Life sucked!

Okay. Skip the snack. Time for some action!

It was almost 11:00 p.m. but she grabbed her keys and a lightweight jacket by the front door, selected tennis shoes over flip flops and tied them tight enough to cut off all blood supply, then locked up and headed out. Out where she hadn't decided yet.

She turned right out of her driveway, forcing herself up Killer Hill, which rose at about a 45 degree angle. Running was impossible, so Logan powered forward as best she could. One foot in front of the other, she climbed until her thighs burned and she was breathing heavily.

She made it to the top. Now that she'd stopped, she felt the drop in temperature. The air was muggy. A fine blanket of mist from a threatening rainstorm settled on her cheeks and eyelids. Wind whistled through eucalyptus branches high overhead.

It suited her mood just fine. She turned around and headed back down toward the beach. Her thighs were relieved, but her knees objected to the steep decline.

Everyone else had the sense to be inside this time of night. Rich, yellow light glowed out from around the edges of curtains and blinds, glimpses of what she was sure were all happy, loving couples and families tucked into secure homes.

She continued down the hill, reveling in the wet, salt on her lips, her hair almost drenched by the time she got to the ocean. With a strong shiver, she pulled up her collar, fumbled with the zipper of her coat, finally yanking it all the way up to her chin, and shoved her hands deeper into the pockets. In the right one, she felt the small can of mace her brother had insisted she carry for safety.

"I'd probably spray *myself* with it if I ever tried to use it," she grumbled in self-pity.

The storm was gearing up in force and volume.

"I'm washable," she said, defying the gods.

Few cars were out, so she jaywalked across the highway to the sand, not waiting for the light. Tava'e's was closed. Only the gas station showed signs of life. No one but a kid reading a magazine behind the counter, haloed by one overhead light.

The wind, no longer blocked by houses and trees, grew stronger and louder out on the deserted beach. A blast of it made her eyes water and her nose run. She found a wad of Kleenex in her other pocket to take care of her eyes and nose. She also found a stale chocolate mint.

Too late, she realized it was probably from the Italian restaurant they'd been to the night Jack died. A flood of memories returned. She pulled it out of her pocket and threw it into the surf, wishing she had the shoebox currently buried in the back of her closet with her so she could throw that in, too, along with the woman who delivered it.

Digging her shoes deeper into the sand, Logan stubbornly braced herself against the wind, her frustration matching each new monster wave crashing on the rocks.

"Shit!"

Rain pelted her face, mingling with her tears. She shoved her fists deeper into her pockets until her knuckles couldn't go any farther without ripping out the seams.

Summer storms are brief in Southern California, so before she was really ready, the wind and waves died down and there was nothing left to do but turn her back on the ocean and trudge up the beach toward home, depositing the now useless Kleenex in one of the trash barrels the city had scattered optimistically along the beach. She really wished the storm had lasted longer, she wasn't done feeling crappy. And she still had to walk back up Killer Hill to get home.

Thirty minutes later, warmed by a hot shower, ready for bed, her head was clearer. She resolved to tackle her problems one at a time, fresh in the morning, starting with scheduling a visit to Howard Miller's glassblowing school, where Elizabeth had lived, along with the other apprentices, Matt, Jared, and his girlfriend, Leah.

Miller might know something more about Elizabeth. He had been her boss, after all, her mentor. The police must have talked with him already, but she hadn't. Now that she thought about it, maybe she'd even have a chance to talk with a certain hotheaded glassblower while she was there. The one she'd seen arguing with Elizabeth a week before her death.

36

Logan realized she had only one clean top—not her favorite—and a pair of jeans to wear. Before she could solve crimes, she needed to do some laundry. She had a few hours to kill anyway, before the office would be open at the glassblower's school.

She was still waiting on a part for her washer and dryer the guy said he needed to finish the installation. Why he hadn't brought it with him the first time was beyond her. He said it was coming in on the next truck out from Riverside. Hopefully, she'd be spinning and drying within the week.

In the meantime, she piled laundry onto the sheets and tied them up like stork packages, threw them into Lola and headed to the local *Spin 'n Fluff*. She found two washers, loaded them up, and settled in with a cold Coke from the vending machine. Hopefully, this wouldn't take long.

When it was time to switch, she was reminded that wet laundry weighs ten times as much as dirty laundry and maintains a wolverine-like grip on the interior walls of the washer. Logan tried not to grunt or grimace during the process, but the pulling motion was a quick and severe reminder that her back was still not a hundred percent. Most of the time she could forget about it, but that old L4/L5 disc was not a happy camper if you pulled on it from certain angles.

Once she was sure she got all of it out, she pushed the awkward cart over to the wall dryers and pushed the heavy bundles in.

"Those dryers only have two settings: Hellfire and Igloo." Logan looked up in time to see a young woman standing next to her, unloading several black net and silver-studded items of clothing from her dryer. No Calvin Klein here. Everything looked like it came from an Army Navy store. She wasn't sure, but Logan thought she'd seen her outside Tava'e's delivering to-go orders to some guys on motorcycles.

"Thanks for the warning," Logan said. She started to add ". . . I don't think I have much choice until my dryer gets hooked up" but thought better of it, since this girl may not have the option of improving her laundry lot anytime soon. Instead, she held out her hand and introduced herself.

"Hi, I'm Logan. Any suggestions for preventing total wardrobe meltdown?"

"Hi," the young woman said, giving Logan's extended hand a firm shake, "Epiphany. Not much, really . . . about the only thing you can do is stop it before the timer says they're done and set it to fluff for the last five minutes. Sometimes that works."

"I'll try that. Thanks."

Bored and hot, spotting a sandwich place across the parking lot, Logan added, "How 'bout if I pay you back for your excellent advice with an iced coffee or something?" nodding her head in the direction of the sandwich shop.

Epiphany thought for a second, then shrugged.

"I could eat."

Over lunch, which consisted of a chopped salad for Logan and a pastrami-on-rye for Epiphany, Logan learned that Epiphany's mother had been a late-blooming flower child with a strange sense of humor. Since Epiphany's father did not stick around to temper her name selection, the young mother gave her only daughter her unusual moniker just so she could say she "*had an Epiphany.*"

"She loved telling people that story," Epiphany said, wiping mustard off her lip, maintaining admirable control of the gargantuan sandwich.

"I considered changing it," she said matter-of-factly, as she swallowed another big bite, "but then she went and got cancer, so I left it. I hope she's still getting as big a kick out of it now, as when she was alive."

There wasn't anything Logan could think of that would be an appropriate response to a story like that, so she just paid the bill.

They didn't get back in time to try Epiphany's fluffing trick, so they just folded Logan's severely wrinkled clothing as best they could and put the piles in her car.

Epiphany was already on her bike, "You live up Killer from Tava'e's, right?"

"Yes, I just moved in a few weeks ago," Logan said.

"Yeah, I've seen your car. Nice ride. You should come down sometime, meet the boss," Epiphany said.

"I've been planning to," Logan said, "My neighbor, Ben, brought me one of those great cinnamon rolls and the coffee was excellent."

"Yeah, Ben's a good guy," she said, making sure her laundry was secure in the saddlebags on the back, checking the buckles.

"You'll like Tava'e. She's helped a lot of us out. Still does," Epiphany added.

Before Logan had time to ask her who Tava'e helped out or the hows and whys, Epiphany added over her shoulder as she gunned her bike, "See you around!"

For some reason, Logan felt she'd just passed the midterm but still had to pass the final, and oddly, she wanted to earn the approval of this girl, who lived life by her own rules and seemed not to care what the world thought.

Epiphany brought to mind a line from Emerson's essay "Self Reliance" in American Lit, something about everyone prattling and playing to get a baby's attention, while the baby acted truly from its own spirit. Babies just let out a holler when they wanted something, without amending their behavior to please others.

When was it that adults stopped expressing their own needs so honestly?

She was still trying to figure out what her needs were. Right now, her own needs were not foremost in her mind, Thomas and Lisa's were. When she got home, now that mundane matters like laundry and lunch were taken care of, Logan called to see if she could schedule a time to talk to Howard.

37

"**G**ood Morning, Sunshine!" Logan bent down to pick up her monster kitten. Things did always look brighter in the morning.

Dimebox had long since earned hardwood floor privileges, having neatly done his business in the cat box for weeks. Yesterday, after making her appointment with Howard—he had answered himself, said he'd be at the school tomorrow afternoon and could see her then—she'd stocked up on a few basics at the local market. Yogurt, eggs, a fragrant loaf of French bread, peanut butter, fresh fruit and veggies, some grapefruit juice, and a good-looking rib-eye. A couple of bottles of decent wine rounded out her purchases. Logan was a quality, not quantity, kind of girl.

After a quick breakfast of peanut butter spread on a hunk of French bread, washed down with grapefruit juice, Logan did what little housework there was to do and took inventory of her remaining home-improvement projects. Coffee maker. She kept forgetting.

She'd also need something to cover the back upstairs window. Some sort of curtains or blinds. If nothing else, she'd tack up a sheet temporarily. She measured the window, scribbled some notes, and trotted downstairs to find her purse and car keys.

Dimebox snoozed in a long parallelogram of sunlight, stretched out on the hardwood floor. Pushing her feet into flip-flops, Logan set off to find a hardware store.

Ben recommended one near the gas station. Maybe she could kill two birds with one stone. Lola was thirsty. She would explore that end of town while she was at it—so much had changed since she lived here last—and grab something to eat after a walk on the beach. It was a little warm already, but she needed to stretch her legs. Tomorrow she'd have to get out earlier.

Several hours later she was back, blinds ordered and WD-40 in hand. The blinds would be in next week. Tonight, she'd just tack up a sheet. Almost dinnertime.

Having never gotten the hang of lighting, let alone cooking on, a BBQ, she'd opted for an indoor George Foreman grill. It worked just fine for flying solo. Plug it in, toss on some meat, and voilà! Dinner in less than five minutes.

She pulled her steak out of the fridge and reached for a bottle of red wine, when Ben knocked on the door. Purgatory sat politely at his side, gazing at her solemnly.

"I came to see if you found everything you needed at Aces. Also to see if you were in the mood for some dinner. I BBQed some bratwurst and made too much for just Purgatory and me."

Keeping direct eye contact with Ben, Logan surreptitiously pulled the dishtowel over her steak on the counter.

"Great minds must think alike, Ben. I was just about to open some wine. If red sounds good to you, I'll bring it over. Syrah okay? And yes, I found everything I needed. You gave great directions." She gestured to her to-do list. "They'll be getting a lot of my business this summer."

Ben nodded his approval on both the time and the wine.

"Be there in five—I just have to make sure Dimebox has food and water first."

"Purgatory and I will be there," he called back, crossing her back yard, stepping over the low hedge between their properties easily.

Logan noted his wide shoulders as he walked away.

Down girl! No messing around with the neighbors.

She popped her steak in a zip lock baggie and tossed it back into the fridge. "Steak and eggs for breakfast!"

Splashing cold water on her face, she ran a brush through her hair, then deftly divided her unruly waves into three sections, twisted them into a loose French braid and changed into something warmer.

"This is *not* a date," she told Dimebox, as the kitten mewed disapprovingly at being left again.

Logan thoroughly enjoyed the evening. It was perfect sweater weather, not too hot, not too cold. Later, after she and Ben polished off two bratwurst-on-sourdough sandwiches each and were sipping the last of the Syrah in front of the built-in fire pit in his back yard, she discovered how Purgatory had earned his name.

The bratwurst, apparently the dog's favorite food since he inhaled three, did not reciprocate in kind. After fighting their way through his digestive system, the brats emerged in lethal farts impossible to ignore. She swore they were strong enough to make her eyes water. Ben profusely apologized, but said it was the dog's only flaw.

Logan made a mental note not to have them over for an inside dinner anytime soon. At least outdoors they had the chance of avoiding asphyxiation! But she had to admit the dog was sweet.

"She keeps me company on my jobs and makes a great foot warmer. My sister or Taylor keeps her if I ever have to go anywhere she can't come."

From what she could gather, he'd taken over his grandfather's landscaping business in town. As she listened to him talk about his life and the changes in Jasper since she'd left, Logan reminded herself to keep Ben firmly in the friend column. The last thing she needed this summer was complications. Tomorrow was another rehearsal with Ned, and she planned on fitting in a trip to see Howard at his glassblowing school, so she thanked Ben for the dinner and the company and took herself home.

"Moon's pretty bright. Can you see your way okay, or do you need me to turn on the light?" Ben asked as she left.

"No, I'm good. Thanks again for dinner."

Ben watched her navigate her way across the two back yards, until she was safely inside. Noting how well her jeans fit, he enjoyed the job.

38

Murder didn't deter the festival crowds. The Otter Festival was back up and busy as ever. Lisa wasn't feeling up to coming in. Her lupus was acting up. Thomas' nephews were down for the powwow, so Logan had the afternoon off, although she did have to play that night. She figured she could do more to help Lisa and Thomas by figuring out who murdered Elizabeth than by working at the booth. The nephews said they could hold down the fort for a few hours, no problem.

Logan hoped to catch Howard by himself. If he had anything to share, it wouldn't be around his students. The glassblowing school didn't show up on GPS, but one of the ticket takers in the front gave her directions.

"That's where his office is, and all the interns live out there, too: Matt, Jared, Leah, and well, until," here she turned red, "well, you know, the other girl, the one who died. She lived there too.

"They're just like dorm rooms, really," the woman confided, eager to cover her embarrassment and change the subject, "I don't think they even have air conditioning or anything. Shared bathrooms and makeshift kitchen. The kids are just grateful to have Howard take them on.

"He's that famous, you know!" she'd concluded, feeling pleased she could end the conversation on a cheerful note.

As she followed the map the woman had drawn, Logan wondered again if Elizabeth had any family, if anyone had come for her. She still couldn't quite come to grips with the fact that this young, vibrant life had been quelled so completely.

She also wondered how the other glassblowers were taking it. Matt obviously had strong feelings toward her—although extremely negative ones—but love and hate are often two sides of the same coin. From what she overheard of their argument, those feelings sounded as much personal as professional. At the very least, he was fiercely competitive, as was Elizabeth.

She had a feeling Matt would not take kindly to rejection by anyone, particularly a beautiful young woman. Had they been involved and, if so, could Matt have fathered Elizabeth's child? Somehow she couldn't see Elizabeth and Matt together, but she wouldn't put it past Elizabeth to use Matt then blithely discard him when someone better able to help her career came along.

She didn't want to cause trouble for Matt if he was innocent of anything more than being an overbearing jerk, but maybe the police should be looking at him and whatever his relationship with Elizabeth had been, not Thomas.

Elizabeth seemed to be the kind of woman who gathered enemies as easily as admirers and didn't seem to care about either. Who else might she have antagonized in the few short months she'd been here? She was nice enough to Jared, but had no use for Leah. In a word, Elizabeth could be described as efficient. She didn't go out of her way to be cruel to anyone, but simply ignored people, as if they didn't exist, unless she needed something from them.

With summer tourist traffic it took about twenty minutes driving inland down Paulson before she saw the large, two-story building on her left. Gravel crunched under Lola's tires when she pulled up in front of a generous, wrap-around porch, fronted by wide wooden stairs. Several glass sculptures were scattered here and there, some blending with the landscape or covered by bushes, others standing alone in the strong, afternoon sun.

There was little shade.

Knowing she would face a scalding steering wheel when she came back, Logan didn't bother pulling up the top. Instead, she draped a beach towel over both wheel and seat. She wouldn't be long.

Making sure her cell phone was in airplane mode, she pushed her keys into her purse and mounted the stairs, which creaked with every step.

Walking through open double doors, she admired the oval, beveled glass in the top half of each, wondering if they were original or made recently by the students. It looked original, but she wasn't an expert. She didn't see anyone around.

Once inside, she found herself facing a short flight of stairs going down into an open-air, concrete courtyard about fifty feet square, filled with the same equipment Logan had seen at the festival: a glassblowing furnace, pipes, buckets of water, metal tables. She could hear the furnace, but no one was working at it right now.

A matching set of stairs rose on the opposite side. Facing the courtyard were about a dozen doors, a few on each side, evenly spaced, making the whole place look a little like a fifties motel, which, in one of its former lives, it had been.

One of the doors, the first one on Logan's left, was open. She could hear Howard on the phone, so walked over to where he could see her, but did not go in so as not to interrupt his conversation. It must have been the former motel office as it still had a reception counter, which partially blocked her view of Howard, sitting at a desk in back, signaling that he'd be right with her.

While she waited, Logan went back to the railing, adjusting her purse on her shoulder, stretching her back. She should have made time for a walk this morning. She'd have to fit a short one in before playing tonight.

Howard had to bend his head down a little when he came out to get her, the door frame having been built for a shorter generation.

39

Reaching out a warm, rough hand to shake hers, Howard apologized for the wait.

"I'm sorry, there has been a lot to do what with . . . everything."

"No worries, I understand," Logan reassured him. "This can't be an easy time for any of you. I appreciate you taking the time to talk with me," she said.

She sat in the offered chair across from Howard as he retook his seat behind his desk.

"You're Thomas' friend."

She waited for him to continue. She was rewarded when Howard turned and focused weary eyes on her own, ". . . just for the record, I don't think Thomas had anything to do with this, so anything I can tell you that might be helpful, I am happy to. Although I don't know anything about the money he gave to Elizabeth. Well, I can guess what she wanted it for, but not why he gave it to her."

News spreads fast in a small town.

Logan decided to let him continue at his own pace. She realized she'd opened a very private door.

He spoke softly, his dove-gray eyes full of pain. Slumped and dispirited, turned halfway toward the window behind him, he began.

"It was a surprise to both of us."

Logan looked around the office while Howard composed himself. It was a pleasant space, rough but functional. The wall behind him was mostly one large window, coming down to a low shelf near the floor, letting in lots of light. She could see the parking lot where Lola was snoozing in the sun. More shelves covered the opposite wall, with lots of technical manuals. A clutch of metal pipes leaned against the wall in the corner. No pictures, but several glass pieces, student work, by the look of them. Blueprints covered the top of his desk. Coffee mugs set on both sides kept them from rolling back up.

Howard himself was weathered, like a classic sailboat with good bones. A few wild, white hairs corkscrewed off his brow, backlit by the afternoon sun. Maybe it was being around artists all day, but Logan saw him as a vintage black and white photo, sitting there, deep in his own thoughts.

Logan remembered when her father began sprouting eyebrow hairs like that. Howard was a good-looking man for his age, but she wondered what a woman as young as Elizabeth would see in him. There must have been at least a thirty-year age difference.

"We knew how it would look," he said, as if in answer to her unasked question, "so we kept it quiet."

"Were things serious?"

"Yes," he replied, without apology. I know how it must sound. Older man, younger woman . . . *much* younger woman. Teacher and student. So cliché, but it wasn't like that." He kept his voice steady.

Logan had learned that if she remained silent, people would keep talking.

"Since my wife died over ten years ago, I just haven't been very social. And I've never been involved with a student."

This last meant to forestall any bad opinion she might have of him for doing just that.

"Elizabeth was different. She was so eager to learn, and so talented. She didn't talk like other young women her age. She didn't spend her time getting her nails done or going out drinking with girlfriends. She didn't have any girlfriends, really. I don't think she liked most women."

Talking about her, he sat up straighter and became animated, "She was entirely focused on her art, on building a life for herself. And she wasn't looking for a sugar daddy. She wanted what I could *teach* her, not what I could *give* her."

Logan continued to listen, trying to do so without judgment.

"She picked up techniques it took me years to learn, and most of my other interns never mastered. She learned in weeks, not months."

"Like Matt for instance?"

"Matt was probably my best student until Elizabeth came." He leaned back in his chair. "But he couldn't hold a candle to her. She was one of a kind."

His voice broke. She knew she should give the man more time but wanted to keep him talking.

"When did Matt find out about you and Elizabeth?"

"About a month ago. I'm afraid Elizabeth laughed about it." He hesitated. "She could be hard, tough—she had a tough life before coming here. I'm afraid she did not let him down gently."

So, Matt definitely had a motive, but did he have an alibi?

"Where was everyone that night?" Logan asked.

"Jared and I are big Quakes fans. Matt's not really into sports, but he drove down to San Diego with us. Leah had a meeting, and Elizabeth doesn't like baseball. She wasn't feeling that great. Said she was going to turn in. The guys and I got back around eleven, called it a night. Everyone tucked into bed by eleven thirty.

Leah and Jared, Logan was surprised to learn, did not share a room.

"Leah belongs to some born-again church," Howard explained, "Works hard, though. To each his own."

Depending on when the actual time of death was, which the ME, according to Rick, couldn't nail down, Matt may or may not be in the clear. She did know Matt made the gruesome discovery of Elizabeth's body the next morning when he opened the annealing oven, where yesterday's pieces had been cooling overnight.

Having seen Elizabeth herself, knowing how it affected her, she couldn't imagine how someone who knew her and had feelings for her must have felt, finding her like that. She was glad it hadn't been Howard.

Still, Matt could have gone to the festival later that night—he had the keys to open the next morning—and argued with Elizabeth again, like he did the other day in the break area, but this time, losing control.

There was nothing more to be learned from Howard. He didn't know of any contact Elizabeth had with anyone from her past. The only mail she'd received was from the couple she knew back east who'd recommended her to Howard, and they'd been nothing but happy for her. In fact, they were flying out for the service.

She assumed Howard had contacted them. She wouldn't want to be the one to make that phone call. According to him, they'd been more like family to her than her real family had been. They located Elizabeth's mother and Howard offered to fly her out, but she said she was too distraught to travel.

Finally, Howard seemed to realize he'd been rambling, roused himself, and stood to walk Logan out. She thanked him for his time. He shook her hand awkwardly, perhaps realizing how personal their conversation had become.

Mumbling something about letting her know when the funeral would be and needing to get back to the festival, he ducked just in time not to hit his head on the door frame on his way out. She wondered how many times he'd missed. He nodded to Matt, who must have come in while they were talking and had just picked up the phone on the counter. It seemed to be the only landline in the place.

Logan decided not to follow Howard out to the parking lot just yet, but to linger a minute and see if she could talk to Matt as long as she was already here. She couldn't wait to see what he had to say for himself.

40

Ignoring Logan, Matt put the phone on speaker, tapping a pen impatiently on the counter. He put her in mind of a simmering volcano.

After listening to what sounded like an anxious customer inquire about a piece being shipped, Matt cut them off mid-sentence and told them their bowl would be packaged, crated for shipping, and sent out in tomorrow's mail.

"Will it get there before we are arriving home? Sweden is far you know," a woman's voice asked.

Matt clipped, "It will get there when it gets there."

"But we are getting home the week next, and we will be needing it for my mother's birthday on the . . . "

"I said it will be there, it will be there!" Matt hung up before she could ask any more questions.

Mr. Congeniality.

Logan cleared her throat and dove in before she lost her nerve, "Hi, Matt, I don't know if you remember me, but my name . . . "

He looked up, as if just realizing she was standing there.

"Logan," he supplied, curious enough to wait and see what she wanted.

"Yes," she responded, surprised he remembered her name.

"You work with Thomas," he added.

"Yes, and I wanted to come by and express my . . . our, condolences about Elizabeth. I know you all worked together closely."

His eyes clouded for a moment, with what must have been a horrible memory. In spite of his demeanor, she felt sorry for him.

"They arrested that Indian guy, Thomas, didn't they? I mean, he's the main suspect, right?" he stated flatly.

So much for compassion.

"I was with him all weekend," Logan said, "We were at the powwow out in Oakdale. He couldn't have been in two places at once," she added, any bit of pity she felt for Matt eclipsed by his arrogant attitude.

Logan watched his reactions. If Matt killed Elizabeth, he would, of course, want to point the finger at someone else.

"Hmmph," Matt said, then turned his back to her and busied himself with some paperwork.

She decided to push a little.

"I was actually surprised to see you at work this week, seeing as how you and Elizabeth had been pretty close. Discovering her . . . well, it must have been awful."

Matt narrowed his gaze at her for a few seconds, sizing her up, before deciding to answer. A nasty smile smeared across his face.

"Well, aren't you the little ghoul?"

"I didn't mean it like that," Logan said.

"Like what?" Matt demanded.

Deciding subtlety and tact were wasted on this guy, Logan took a more direct approach.

"I know you cared for Elizabeth, and I know she didn't feel the same way. I heard you arguing with her. I heard what she said to you, *and* what you said back."

He leveled a scathing look in her direction.

"If you're trying to pin this on me just to get Thomas off the hook, you're *way* off base. I don't waste my time with skanks like her. Once I found out she was banging Howard . . ."

Having just learned from Howard about his relationship with Elizabeth, she wasn't surprised at the information, but at the venom with which it was spewed.

" . . . Yeah, I bet you didn't know that little tidbit," he said, "Once I found out her tastes ran to older, rich guys who could help her get ahead, I didn't waste another second of my time. I make a mistake once, not twice. She was history. I hadn't talked to her for at least two weeks; ask anyone. When I make a decision, I stick to it."

With that, he turned his back on her.

Interview over.

*****

Leaving Matt to pull wings off flies or whatever it was he did with his afternoons, Logan glanced at her watch and walked back to her car. The steering wheel was, as predicted, hot enough to brand mastodons, but the beach towel she'd thrown across the seat saved the backs of her thighs from sizzling when she got in.

She wasn't sure how much of his last claim to believe, but the conversation with Matt had taken longer than she expected, and she needed to get back to the Festival by 6:00 p.m. No time for a run today. She just had time to get to the Otter

Festival, park, and swing by to check on the booth before the first set.

When she got there, Lisa was shooing her nephews out. Said she felt well enough to come in for a few hours and close. The booth traffic slowed down in the evenings. Don't worry about her. She'd be fine. After dinner, most festival goers congregated around the courtyard for food and music.

Logan was pleasantly surprised to see a smile on Lisa's face and something resembling hope in her eyes. She joined her behind the display counter, so they could talk with some privacy.

"He called," Lisa spoke in an excited whisper, although her nephews had already left and there were no customers at the moment.

"Who? Thomas?"

"No, the investigator! Mr. Woodrow. He says he might have some good news and that he'll get in touch soon. Thomas may be able to come home tomorrow if he calls tonight. There will be no more reason for him to stay quiet, protecting me, once they realize he had no reason to kill Elizabeth."

Logan's shoulders relaxed and she hugged her friend, although she wasn't sure Lisa's hope was entirely justified yet.

"That's great news! Call me when you know for sure, okay?"

"Okay, and thanks—for everything."

Just then a couple asked to see something in the case, so their conversation was cut short. Even so, Logan walked away feeling grateful for at least an inkling of good news.

As she made her way to the back stage and tuned up, she mulled over the remaining unanswered questions. There were many. Luckily, when she began playing, the music did its usual magic and, after a rough start, temporarily quieted the tangled puzzles running around in her brain.

SHATTERED

Playing forced her brain and body to work together, bringing her back into focus, into balance, kind of like what Lisa talked about. Maybe that's what everyone needed—to be brought back into balance.

For Logan, playing her violin did the job. For this gift from her great-grandmother, via her father, she was always grateful.

41

Hitting their stride, Logan and the rest of the band could have played all night, but Iona kicked everybody out by nine, so they only did one encore before packing it in. They were scheduled to play again tomorrow, so didn't need to break everything down completely. After looking at the latest pictures of Quinn on Sally's phone in the parking lot, Logan hugged her friends and promised to have them over sometime soon to meet Ben.

Ned watched until she was safely in her car. Logan waved back and followed them out of the back gate. When they reached PCH, she took a right and headed home.

Checking her mirrors first, seeing there was almost no traffic, Logan allowed herself the wicked luxury of sneaking the speedometer up past seventy, breathing in the rush of cold, salty air.

But later that night, as if in punishment for this moment of unguarded joy, Logan dreamed of the accident. Her memories of that night were spotty at best, except for one clear picture she wished she could forget.

It was the moment she knew Jack was dead. The very alive Jack Morgan. Dead. She knew because she saw everything clearly—too clearly—from where she had been thrown clear of the Jeep when it rolled.

No siren sounded and no red lights whirled urgently when the ambulance that held his body slowly pulled away from the curb.

The rest of that night was a sepia-toned blur, a garbled soundtrack cutting in and out, but that moment was captured in full color, forever framed and mounted on the walls of her mind.

Unable to go back to sleep, Logan lay awake, thinking of everything that had happened since then. She'd been so busy dealing with everything, she hadn't actually processed any of it. Maybe that's why her subconscious was pushing these memories forward now. Maybe it was time.

*****

She didn't remember much about the first few days, except walking numbly through the foreign territory of 'making arrangements.'

First, she had to reach their daughter, Amy. She finally located her through a Doctors Without Borders crew, working in a nearby village. Logan wanted to be there, wanted to hold her daughter when she told her, but all she could do was hold the phone tightly and listen to her daughter sob, over three thousand miles away.

One of the doctors gave Amy a ride to Nairobi, and after several long flights, she arrived the day before her father's funeral.

The girl who got off the plane was a pale copy of the carefree, twenty-one-year-old spitfire she and Jack had driven to the airport just a few months before. Amy had gone to Africa to gather photographs of women for a book one of her professors was writing, but got involved in something new. Logan wished she could erase the grief her father's death plainly etched on her daughter's face.

The funeral was packed. Jack had so many friends. The entire company turned out, clients, neighbors, people she'd never seen before and, of course, his rugby team. Outgoing and full of energy, Jack played hard and worked hard, dancing easily through life, everyone only too happy to follow his lead.

Over breakfast the next morning, and during long walks in the following days, Amy told her mother of the work she was doing. The photography project, which was about documenting the exotic women of various African tribes, morphed into something much more meaningful and political.

Amy met a group of women who had transformed their village, economically and socially, after becoming involved in the Green Belt movement.

"It's amazing what they accomplished, Mom. With nothing! Just planting trees! This woman named Wangari Maathai, started it all. She won the Nobel Peace prize."

Logan envied the resilience of youth, as the pent-up energy and enthusiasm poured out of her daughter. She could see so much of all the good parts of Jack in their child.

"Did you know Africa used to be green? At least, a lot of it was. I want to help, Mom. I want to go back."

Amy looked down at her hands, her strawberry blonde bangs skimming almost invisible brows. Logan pictured the hot, African sun beating down on her daughter's fair skin.

"I can't just sit here, feeling bad about Daddy." She paused, "I need to work, but I need to know you'll be okay."

Logan knew if she asked, her daughter would stay, and she wanted nothing more than to have a few more weeks with her, but as much as she wanted that, she knew it would not be good for Amy. Her daughter needed to be in motion. She was a McKenna woman, after all.

So, two weeks later, with her mother's blessing and a new laptop so they could do video calls, the youngest, independent McKenna was on a plane to New York, then on another heading back to Kenya. They would keep in touch whenever Amy could get to a fast enough internet connection.

For the first few months after Bonnie and Mike took her in, Logan slowly graduated from numb to functioning, at least to the outside world. A decision had to made about the business. Until the accident, the company took up most of her life. She enjoyed starting and growing the company with Jack. But after his death, her heart just wasn't in it.

Maybe it never was. A music major in college, it wasn't her dream to start a computer company. Why hadn't she continued with music? Jack would not have held her back.

"Just because you *can* run a business, doesn't mean you *have* to run a business," Bonnie observed one night when they were watching a rerun of "When Harry Met Sally."

She'd never thought of that.

Logan was kind of stumped. The only thing she did know was that it was time to get a life, which included a job and a place of her own to live. A sixth grade teacher at a nearby school, Bonnie nudged her out of indecision, and into taking the sub job at Roosevelt in Tilcott. Next came the purchase of her new home, a continual work-in-progress.

"It's just for a year," Bonnie said, "a long-term sub job. Seventh grade. If you like it, you can stay. I don't think Melanie's coming back, but even if she does, they always have openings at the middle school—not very many people can handle hormonal pre-teens. If you don't like it, there's no obligation to come back in the fall."

Sounded like a win/win. Logan figured it was a stopgap measure until she figured out what she wanted to do with the rest of her life. She hadn't counted on falling for the kids. Or any of what came next.

Because of her spartan living arrangements at Bonnie's, Logan moved into her new home with only her violin, Bella, a good bed, a copy of Kahlil Gibran's "The Prophet," a couple of boxes of Amy keepsakes, and a small book of wise sayings with the tongue-in-cheek title of "A Guide for the Advanced Soul" that Thomas had given her years ago. Her clothes, a Royal Doulton teacup her mom drank strong Earl Gray from every morning until she left, and a toothbrush were also added in. It all fit in her car.

Logan sold most everything from her and Jack's townhouse, reducing her extra baggage to the disturbing pink shoebox, whose lid was secured firmly with a thick rubber band. It was still in the back of her closet behind her boots. There would be time to deal with it later.

42

Cool mornings were one of the perks of living near the beach. Taking full advantage of the warm cocoon of cotton quilts piled on top of her, Logan snuggled in deep. She needed another hour of sleep, but the bright sun streaming in the window drove all possibility of additional slumber out of the room. At least it also pushed last night's dreams back into the shadows of her mind.

Today's worries, however, were front and center. She lay there taking mental inventory. Even if Thomas was cleared, that would put the spotlight right back on Danny, who had no alibi and was connected somehow to a robbery up in Portland. She still didn't think Danny was capable of violence of any kind, but they'd said drugs were involved. She hadn't seen Danny in years. He probably wasn't the sweet little boy she remembered.

But someone had killed Elizabeth and they should be held responsible. It offended Logan's sense of justice that the real culprit was out there somewhere, getting away with murder. You'd think they would have suspected Matt. They must have discovered his unfriendly relationship with Elizabeth by now, and they'd questioned everyone, hadn't they? But he'd been with Howard and Jared at the game until eleven that night. He and Jared shared a room. He said Jared would be able to verify that he didn't go anywhere until he left to go set up around 8:00 a.m.

Rose, the weaver from Oregon, had shared her very definite opinions with her and Lisa last week that she still believed it was Neva's son, Danny, who was guilty.

"I don't care how innocent those street kids look, when you get drugs involved, they're capable of anything. I can't tell you how many times I had to step over dirty panhandlers just to open my shop in the morning when I lived in Portland. And when they're high, there's no reasoning with them. They'll attack you for the change in your pocket. I've seen five cops try to stuff one guy into the back of a police car when he was out of his mind on drugs. That's one of the reasons I moved to Lincoln City. It's too cold for them there, and there's no Pioneer Square for them to panhandle in."

She continued, "In fact, that explains why so many things have gone missing around here, that boy probably sold them for drugs."

Several vendors had complained about some thefts, but it was probably inevitable you'd have some shoplifting in any festival. Someone was stealing, but that didn't mean it was Danny.

It rubbed Logan the wrong way when someone made blanket assumptions. Not all kids did drugs, first of all, even homeless kids, and not all drugs made you violent. And no one knew for sure if Danny was involved in drugs at all, or if he was guilty of anything other than being in the wrong place at the wrong time at that liquor store up in Oregon. On the other hand, she hadn't seen Danny in a long time, and didn't know him that well when he was here. He was just always part of the landscape. Everyone knew Danny, but none of them really *knew* Danny. Anything was possible.

Logan's growling stomach brought her back to the present. They hadn't released Danny when the ME found the obsidian knife tip buried under Elizabeth's rib cage. He was still being held until the Portland police could send someone down. Rick said no one had been formally charged, though, so who knew what the police were thinking. Was it forty-eight or seventy-two hours the police could hold someone without formally charging them? She'd have to catch up on her *Law and Order* reruns.

Whatever the status, until, when, and if Lisa's investigator came through, Thomas and Danny were both still on the hook. Danny was probably unable to really understand what was going on, let alone defend himself, and Thomas *wouldn't* defend himself, trying to protect Lisa.

Hunger calling, she threw off the covers, shook them out over the bed, and propped her lone pillow up against the wall. Simple. No tucking in needed.

Lisa didn't need her 'til one o'clock, so she still had plenty of time for a quick beach walk and breakfast before going over to talk to Jared.

A couple of soft-boiled eggs and another slice of baguette later, Logan was brushing seedpods and pollen off Lola's ragtop. Apologizing again for having to leave her outside, Logan opened the door and slid into the driver's seat. The interior was still cool, thanks to the eucalyptus and jacaranda sheltering the rutted drive.

The sapphire beauty started up like a champ, anticipating the open road. Putting on her sunglasses, Logan backed her onto the street and headed down the hill. Turning left onto PCH, she eased into morning traffic, pointing her car toward the glassblowers' compound. Jared had called and asked if she could come out there instead, as he wasn't going into the festival today.

As she drove, she remembered what Rick said they discovered at the autopsy, about Elizabeth being five weeks pregnant, and again wondered whose baby it was, and if she or anyone had known.

Somehow, Elizabeth didn't seem the type to have an unexpected pregnancy. She was too cool and, it appeared, calculating for that. Wouldn't a pregnancy get in her way? It didn't seem to fit with her very definite career plans. Internship with Howard, Chihuly workshop, win contest, blackmail Thomas to get money to open up her own shop. Check, Check, Check! That was her timeline. Where did pregnancy fit in? It seemed like a very mundane circumstance for such a single-minded person to allow.

It must be Howard's baby, but if he knew, he hadn't mentioned it, and somehow she thought he would have. It could have been Matt's. She wasn't sure how intimate Matt and Elizabeth's relationship had been. Or Matt could just have been angry it was Howard's and not his, which would bring him right back up to number one on the suspect list. She wasn't sure who knew Elizabeth had been pregnant, if anyone.

The more she knew, the less she understood what had really happened that night.

43

The only people she hadn't talked with yet were Jared and his girlfriend, Leah. She hoped this wasn't a wasted trip. They all lived on the compound. Maybe they saw something or heard something. Maybe Jared could at least alibi Matt. And if he couldn't, well, that would make Matt a lot more interesting as a suspect.

The single, stand-alone glassblowing furnace, though unattended, roared in the back left corner of the courtyard. Several metal tables framed the area. The set-up was similar to the glassblowing demo cage at the festival. Racks of poles, metal, and wood instruments and a couple of buckets littered the floor. A skinny green hose snaked along the concrete floor, wrapped around the legs of a wooden bench in front.

Jared appeared to be napping when Logan arrived. Feet up, stretched full-length on a ratty couch on the far, right side of the courtyard, just away from the heat of the furnace, hat pulled loosely down over his eyes. Only the bottom half of his face could be seen. The armpits of his t-shirt were stained with sweat. Logan hesitated, not wanting to wake him up. Men looked so vulnerable when they slept, like overgrown boys. Her maternal instincts kicked in and she wanted to pull a blanket over him and make sure he ate his vegetables.

She smiled at her easy slide into mother mode and wondered how Amy was doing just then. With a nine-hour time difference, she was probably asleep herself.

Several of the doors along the walkway above the courtyard were open, trying to catch a non-existent breeze. She wondered which rooms each of them lived in, and if Howard lived there too, or had a house somewhere else. Camouflage netting stretched across the top of the quad. Were they expecting air strikes? She supposed it provided a little bit of shade.

While waiting for Jared to wake up, she looked around. All quiet on the home front. Howard wasn't in his office today, and Matt wasn't barking at anyone on the phone.

Logan cleared her throat, hoping to wake Jared gently.

Before she could say anything, an insistent voice whispered loudly in her left ear, "He's *resting*!"

Logan about jumped out of her skin. Leah had come up behind her. She urgently motioned for Logan to come back toward Howard's office and the parking lot to avoid waking Jared. Her glasses, which Logan had never seen her wear before, had thick lenses and made her look owlish.

She stepped back to regain her equilibrium and some personal space.

"Hello Leah, I have an appointment with Jared. He's expecting me."

"He's *resting*!" Leah stage whispered again, a little more insistently, pushing her glasses up her nose, as if maybe Logan hadn't heard or understood her the first time.

"Okay, I can talk to you for a little while, until he wakes up."

Momentarily taken aback, Leah hesitated a second, then answered, "Well, I guess so. What do you want to talk to me about?"

"Well, I . . . "

"Leah?" Jared said, rubbing his head groggily.

He got his bearings and motioned for them to come downstairs and join him.

"Logan, right? Sorry, I must have dozed off.

He pulled up a small, metal café chair for her, from a cluster of spares facing the furnace, behind a velvet theater rope, used for observation she supposed, then sat down across from the couch. Leah sat next to Jared on the other side, folding her hands in her lap.

Before Logan could ask any questions, Leah jumped in.

"Jared's been really busy getting ready for the Finnish International! Howard's sending him," she beamed. "We're going to Africa!" she added.

"Oh!" Leah said, jumping up, "I almost forgot! I was just bringing your water when *she* came," giving Logan a look that let her know she saw her visit as an intrusion.

From somewhere in her voluminous, multi-pocketed overalls, she pulled out a clear plastic water bottle. Lemon slices floated near the top.

"You've got to keep hydrated."

"Thanks, hon." He accepted the water bottle and when she kept looking at him, took a swig, thanking her with a wan smile. As an extra gesture, he rubbed the back of her neck, "She takes good care of me, my girl."

Satisfied, Leah relaxed back in the couch.

Logan had no idea how Africa figured into the Finnish competition but didn't want the conversation to veer off on a tangent. She figured it was up to her to get the conversation back on track, even as she began wondering why she came.

She wasn't a detective, and there was really no reason to be bothering these people with her questions. She plowed ahead just to get it over with, determined this was the last digging she'd be doing. Maybe someday she'd learn to mind her own business.

"Is this the big competition you and Elizabeth were talking about the other day? You were going to help her get ready for it?" Logan asked Jared, hoping Leah wouldn't answer for him again.

"Yeah, and she would have been ready, too. She was going for a record, remember?" Jared's energy seemed to pick up.

"Yes, she talked about that. The biggest piece a woman had ever done?" Logan remembered, from the conversation they'd shared on the bench by the tree after Elizabeth's demo.

"Biggest piece *anyone* ever blew—and she would have done it, too. She was small, but those arms! Man, she was strong— stronger than any woman I've ever met."

Leah cleared her throat.

"Well, except for my Leah here. She tosses those bags of sand around like they're bean bags."

This earned him another beaming smile from Leah, who looked for the world, just then, more Golden Retriever than girlfriend.

So as not to leave the girl out again, she addressed both of them, "You worked with Elizabeth. Did either of you notice anything different about her? Had she been acting any different way, or had anyone come to visit her? Did she receive any mail or phone calls that might indicate someone from her past may have done this?"

Leah looked at Jared, and Jared shook his head, "No, I worked with her last week, and I didn't notice anything. She seemed happier, if anything. Things must have been going really good for her. She must have sold some big pieces and taken some pre-paid orders, because she said she was almost ready to get her own studio. I still can't believe she's dead. It's all so weird."

Logan knew where she got the money but didn't share.

Jared took off his ball cap, wiped his brow and jammed it back on his head.

"Need to get back to it," he told Logan. "I heard the police are close. I sure hope they get the right guy soon. Tell Thomas no one thinks he did it. He's a good guy."

"Yeah," Logan agreed. She thanked both Jared and Leah for their time, graciously accepted a religious pamphlet from Leah, who seemed to have a supply of them in her overalls at all times. This one exclaimed, 'Worry About the Fires of Hell, not Global Warming . . . Trust in God!'

She made her way back out to the parking lot and left them to the rest of their day. Leah was an odd duck, but Jared seemed happy with her.

No more enlightened than when she came, and increasingly frustrated and worried, she got back into her car and buckled up. It was starting to look like she'd be unable to help Thomas before Lisa blurted out her past.

She left the top down, hoping the fresh air would clear her mind. A red-tailed hawk soared above her, and she wished she had as clear a view as he did of the road she was on.

44

It was six o'clock before Logan pulled into the gravel drive. She got out, pulled up the top, giving Lola a pat, reassuring her tonight would be the last night she'd be out in the cold, because the contractor was installing the new garage door tomorrow. As she walked up the path to the front door, she heard Dimebox, mewing loudly for his dinner.

"Keep your fur on!" she said as she turned the key in the lock and let herself in.

Pressing against her ankles as if she'd been gone for months, not hours, he continued to mew, quieter, but still sounding distressed.

"Are you feeling okay?" She picked him up and looked in his eyes. She checked his nose to see if it was wet. Was it dogs who were supposed to have the wet nose, or cats? Or was it a warm nose?

Before she could contemplate the cat mystery any further, she noticed one of the French doors was open about a foot. She put the cat back down on the floor, where he continued to pace. Had she had a break in? It didn't look like anything had been disturbed or taken.

She felt suddenly chilled, her new home less safe. Should she call Rick? Jack used to handle situations like this. This was silly. She could handle this. It was her own fault. She'd just have to lock up better next time.

She went to the kitchen drawer and tossed around for a likely weapon. She pulled out a wrench, the one she used to bang nails in the wall to hang pictures of Amy in the hallway. She'd never actually used a wrench as a wrench but knew the rolling thing in the middle adjusted the width.

Holding it aloft, she put up a brave front, "Wrench Woman! Able to bang big nails into solid studs . . . Able to . . . ," She couldn't think of a second 'able to' but the task kept her occupied long enough to check out all of the closets, the back yard and the upstairs bedroom and bathroom without losing her nerve.

No boogiemen found, she made sure all the windows and doors were locked, chalked it up to early Alzheimer's and changed for bed.

Still wired, she couldn't get to sleep.

She missed Amy. She was so far away. A wave of homesickness for her daughter, mixed with fresh grief over Jack, enveloped her. She suddenly missed all that she and Jack had, and all that they never would have. Even after the pink shoebox revelations, she sometimes missed him so much it physically hurt.

At the same time, irrational images of Amy being attacked by lions, kidnapped, or worse, played across her mind.

Breathing helped. She consciously slowed down her breathing, knowing this wave of anxiety and grief would pass. Rational thought returned as she realized she could not protect Amy thousands of miles away, and that she was probably just fine anyway, and she, Logan, was worried for nothing.

SHATTERED

Logically, she knew Amy could just as easily be attacked on a college campus in California as on a street in Nairobi. She'd taught Amy as much as any parent can in the short time they have with their children before they fly the nest. Now she just had to let her go. That's how her father had raised her, and it made sense. She knew it was best, even though it was painful at times. She wanted her daughter to be free to stretch out and live her life, without being weighed down by fear.

Logan wanted to time travel back to one of their slumber parties, when they ate a whole package of chocolate chip cookies and a pint of Haagen Dazs each, watching Little Mermaid. It usually was just the two of them, she realized. Jack was often traveling, or out with his rugby buddies.

It never occurred to her that other husbands and fathers were different, until she spent time around Bonnie and Mike. When he wasn't at the firehouse, Mike was in the kitchen with Bonnie, working on the garden out back, or crawling around on the floor with the kids, giving brontosaurus rides. He did not feel hemmed in by family, but seemed deeply content.

In hindsight, it was really her and Amy who had made home, home. In many ways, Jack had been just a charming visitor. He swept you off your feet when he was there, though, she had to admit. Everybody adored Jack. Amy still did, and Logan vowed she would never do anything to change that.

45

With a philosophical shrug Logan gathered her laptop, pushed her feet into a pair of flip flops she kept by the door, and shook off any residual nervousness about burglars, break-ins, or less than perfect marriages. Funny, she thought as she closed the French door behind her, she never had worried much about her marriage. Maybe she should have.

With the now mollified Dimebox trotting close beside her, leaping from step to step, she mounted the stairs to her rooftop sanctuary. Easing herself down in her teak deck chair, she retrieved the wine opener from the storage bench, and efficiently twisted the cork out of the bottle. After pouring herself a glass, she burrowed into the chaise lounge and opened her computer, hoping for an email from Amy.

She was rewarded with a good, long one. Although her daughter was a natural story teller, and wrote as easily and voluminously as she talked, she was so busy living her life, she had less and less time to write home about it. Which, Logan supposed, was good.

Amy was creating her own life, thousands of miles away. And, Logan discovered, her new life included a botanist named

Liam, who was helping with the tree project. Amy mentioned Liam more and more, and coming home for Thanksgiving less and less.

"Guess my little girl is growing up," Logan informed Dimebox, who didn't bother to raise his head at this earth-shattering news.

She was halfway through her glass of wine before she clicked on the next email, this one from Bonnie, who was still in Puerto Vallarta with Mike, lounging on the beach, and no doubt draining the place dry of whatever umbrella drinks were being served.

Hey Chiquita!

This is your amiga, Bonita! I'm not even sure that's a word, but I think it means beautiful woman, at least I'm going with that translation! I have some possibly fantastic news. I can't give you the details yet, but due to a small slice of geographic luck, you may have yours truly to thank for some very good *news in the near future, regarding the very* bad *news you received the last day of school—Keep your fingers crossed!*

We'll be back Sunday night, late. Why don't you bring that nice neighbor of yours, the hunky Viking, along with you? Dinner? Monday night around 7? Oh, and of course, Rick and Charlie.

I'll fill you in then!

TTFN

Bonnie

With everything else going on, she'd almost forgotten about the letter bomb she'd received on the last day of school. She still hadn't made a decision to either fight it or drop the whole thing and not go back. The choice they'd given her was to accept the job in the fall but live with a letter in her file questioning her integrity, which any principal who wanted to hire her could read—or look for a new career.

SHATTERED

That all seemed so insignificant now, in light of Thomas and Lisa's problems, but she knew that she also needed to eat and therefore needed a job by September. She could not afford the luxury of ignoring the situation much longer. She'd have to make a decision soon. The problem was there was no way to defend herself, as they weren't saying *how* they thought she cheated, just that due to her students' high test scores, she *must* have.

She'd never been in a situation where she felt so torn. She had no problem walking out on a low-paying, bureaucratic job, working with a bad boss and a petty, manipulative coworker, but she did have a problem walking out on the kids. When it was just her and her students in the classroom, she felt alive, and time fell away. She loved it. Only when she played Bella did she feel the same total engagement and joy. Teaching made her happy.

She had no idea what to do.

Pulling herself back to Bonnie's email, she was curious about her friend's mysterious news. After filling her in on her own recent events, waiting to tell her everything about Thomas and Lisa until she could break the news to her in person, she promised she would be there Monday night for dinner.

She wasn't sure about inviting Ben, yet. Having him meet Bonnie and Mike felt too much like bringing him home to meet her parents. Relationships were so complicated!

Later that night, as she drifted into sleep, her subconscious sorted through the bits and pieces of information she'd gleaned over the last few days. Dreams swirled with disjointed images of knights and pawns, the fiery, red glow of the glassblowers' furnace, dead mice, Howard's sad eyes, and Matt's face, twisted in anger.

Another memory tugged at her, but she couldn't quite reach it. Some small detail . . . no, it was gone. Maybe tomorrow.

46

She'd overslept. Logan hauled herself out of bed, feeling worse off in spite of getting a good eight hours of sleep. Every joint was stiff, her eyes dry and scratchy. She really needed to get a walk in today.

Fingers pressed to her tailbone, bending back until she achieved a satisfying pop, she hoped she wouldn't have to add allergies to her list of physical ailments. Her chiropractor had mentioned she might want to lay off wheat, sugar, and dairy for a while. Said it might clear up her joint stiffness.

Like that was going to happen.

"I will not give up cinnamon rolls," she informed Dimebox as she walked down the stairs, "or baguettes."

Dimebox had no comment. Doubled in weight as well as hunting prowess, he waited patiently for her at the bottom of the stairs, looking satisfied with himself. He obviously wasn't allergic to anything.

Thanks to the cat door she'd installed next to the French doors, he had taken to midnight jaunts, leaving gifts on the back doorstep. This morning's present was a delicate, gray mouse, its body curled on the cold cement in the fetal position.

Lovely.

As big as Dimebox was getting, it'd be a possum next. She fetched a broom and dustpan from the kitchen, opened one of the doors, scooped up the small, pitiful carcass and deposited it into the trash can out back, on top of Leah's religious tract she'd thrown out the night before. How could anyone believe in such a negative version of God? She found herself wondering again if Jared shared her views. He just didn't seem the religious fanatic type.

Not her business.

Offended by her total lack of appreciation of his gift, Dimebox trotted past her, twitching tail held regally aloft.

On her way back into the house, Logan noticed another gift, a plastic bag hung on one of the outside door handles. It hadn't been there last night when she locked up. There was a note taped on the outside of the bag.

For Coffee Emergencies—found this old one laying around, thought you could use it.

Logan opened the bag and peeked inside. A brand new Mr. Coffee pot stuffed with a fragrant bag of freshly ground beans. Ben said it was "an old one," but she knew by the receipt in the bag he'd just bought it. Good to know he wasn't a very good liar. Given recent revelations about Jack, that information was reassuring.

She definitely needed a caffeine boost to finish waking up. She couldn't leave the house anyway with the contractor coming to install the garage door, so she put Ben's gift to good use.

The contractor promised to get there by 10:00 a.m., so she went back inside, read the directions, rinsed it out and made a fresh pot of coffee, settling in to wait. She grabbed a banana from the bowl on the counter. The smell of fresh coffee filled the kitchen. Her little hobbit hole was starting to feel like home.

Burrowing into the couch, which still had that rich feel and smell of new leather, she sipped her second cup and checked her phone. Lots of junk email and a missed call.

There was also a text from Ben, who wanted to make sure she found her care package at the back door, and that Epiphany had ground the newly roasted beans this morning special. Colombian. Logan was learning more about coffee and realized she liked that one. Medium or dark roasts. The light ones just tasted like flavored water.

"If you're around later, maybe we can do some BBQ or walk down to Juan's," he added.

The missed call was from Lisa. Logan decided to call her back first. No answer, so she left a message she'd try again later. Probably still sleeping, poor woman. Maybe the investigator finally called back with good news and she and Thomas were out celebrating.

She decided to check out the job boards this morning. She hadn't made up her mind yet, just wanted to keep her options open. Wouldn't hurt to see what was out there.

47

"How come I got stuck with the dog?"

Don scowled and leaned against the refreshments table while Trevor piled a plate high with brownies and chocolate-chip cookies.

"Aw, come on. She's not that bad, she's just quiet. And she's stacked!"

"She can't even dance. Looks like an albatross having puppies."

This made absolutely no sense, but Trevor said, "Here," slipping a handful of mini airline bottles into his friend's jacket pocket.

"Have some fun. I paid for the tickets. I filled up your car. All you had to do was buy her flowers."

Don adjusted the bottles with a practiced hand, sliding a few to an inside pocket, the same pocket that held his insurance policy, a bottle of small, round, white pills. Never hurt to have backup.

Although he had confidence in the pills, he continued to grouse, making sure Trevor understood he owed him one.

"All I need is a virgin keeping her legs clamped shut all night."

"Look, you can drop me off at Rhonda's. I'll walk home from there. Go by the park. Just get a few drinks in her after you drop us off. She'll loosen up."

"She'd better."

Don grabbed a cookie off the plate and, not bothering to get anything for his date, followed Trevor back to the girls.

He was through with her just before midnight, then drove her home.

He smiled when her mother thanked him for seeing her home safely and walking her to the door. Nobody seemed to notice she had nothing to say.

Her dad was snoring away on the couch. Her mom, unused to waiting up since Leah had never been on a date, yawned and asked her how it was. Did she have a good time?

Leah mumbled something about being tired, and walked quietly upstairs. The shower ran out of hot water in about fifteen minutes, but not until she'd scrubbed her skin raw.

She should have fought. It all happened so fast. He was right. She *was* just a stupid cow. That's what he'd said. He'd been mad at her for "just laying there."

After her shower, she pulled on her long, flannel nightgown, climbed into bed and lay as still as she could under her covers until she knew her mother was asleep, then sneaked downstairs. She tiptoed through the kitchen and very slowly turned the dead bolt on the back door. It opened with a thud, which caused her blood to freeze, but neither of her parents woke. Slowly she started to breathe again. Under cover of a moonless night, she slipped into the alley behind the house and stuffed the hated dress deep into the trashcan, covered securely by a pizza box and a rancid milk carton.

He hadn't even left her underwear. He let her keep her bra (probably because her parents would have noticed that), but laughed and said he was keeping the underwear, threatening to staple it up on the bulletin board outside the office with her name written across it in Sharpie if she told.

She made it back to her bed but couldn't sleep. Her mom kept saying she was so glad she had a good time and what a handsome boy he was.

It was a long weekend.

She dreaded Monday morning. Only two weeks ago, she thought her luck had changed. Rhonda, the new girl who sat next to her in Biology, didn't seem to notice Leah's old-fashioned, ill-fitting clothes, or lack of other friends. Rhonda made friends easily. They moved around a lot, she said, her dad being in the military and all.

Rhonda got her the date. He was her boyfriend's best friend. Her mom got her that awful dress, but the magic Rhonda had worked with her hair almost made up for it. She had been so excited.

Rhonda used pearl combs to lift Leah's hair back off her face, to 'show off your cheekbones'. Not real pearls, of course, but very pretty. Now she couldn't wait to be rid of them. Rhonda had PE first period. Leah walked into the locker room and silently handed her the combs, along with the raspberry lipstick she had borrowed.

"Oh, Leah, you took your hair down! I wanted everyone to see it. You could have left the curls in, you know. They would have looked just as good down. Why'd you brush it all out?"

It was obvious Rhonda didn't know what had happened, and Leah couldn't find the words to tell her, so she just walked away.

"Well, of all the . . . " Rhonda shrugged and turned back to her locker, noting Leah had reverted to her baggy clothes. You could hardly see her face through that wall of hair.

There's just no helping some people.

For the first few months that summer, Leah stumbled around on autopilot. When fall came and everyone else was going off to college, her dad handed her the want ads at breakfast and informed her bluntly she needed to get a job.

There was an opening for a custodian's assistant at the assisted living center run by the Church of the Lamb. The chapel was next door and within weeks, Leah felt more welcome there than she was at home. Realizing she was unwanted at home, she rented a room from Thelma Carter, a recent widow, and was determined to work her way back into God's good graces. She felt the whole prom incident was her fault. She should have said "No!" louder, fought harder.

Two months later, the blood came. It was Sunday and the sermon was half over. She barely made it to the bathroom in time. She thought her period had started, but there was a lot more blood than usual. It frightened her as it kept coming, filling the toilet, and the pain was unbearable. She was alone. It was awful and felt like it would never end.

When it was over, although she was almost too weak to stand, she looked in the toilet and saw a large, bloody clump. Frightened, she flushed it down the toilet, washed her legs off as best she could, stuffed a bunch of toilet paper in her underwear, and forced herself to go back inside.

Hoping no one would notice anything was wrong, she slid into the last pew, waiting to get her strength back before she needed to stand up again.

The preacher was at the end of his sermon now.

SHATTERED

Who can find a virtuous woman? For her price is above rubies. She looketh to the ways of her household . . . .

Leah suddenly felt light, and for the first time since that awful night, a feeling of peace descended on her. God was speaking right to her, telling her what to do.

That was the secret. Service. Work. That's what was needed. That would purify her. Someday maybe she would be worthy to be a helpmeet. She could still be a virtuous woman.

The preacher's wife could see she was pale and shaky when she came back from the bathroom. Assuming she was just suffering from cramps, she drove her to the drugstore for supplies, chatting the whole way.

Leah smiled weakly and allowed her to drive her back to her rented room with a sack of Kotex, Midol and Snickers bars the woman had kindly stopped and purchased for her.

"Tell Thelma to get you fixed up with a hot water bottle, hon. That'll fix you right up. And eat one of those *Snickers* right away when you get in. Chocolate helps everything!"

48

"Leah?" Jared called up to Leah's room on the second floor. "You ready? We're leaving in a few minutes."

In answer, Leah came out of her room, hurrying down the stairs. She was dressed in a soft denim jumper that came just below her knees, with a basic, white t-shirt underneath. Black flats and a large, hobo purse completed her standard church ensemble. The purse, a gift from Jared, was of good quality, supple, brown leather, and on anyone else would be fashionable, but on Leah, it was somehow reduced to mere function.

Jared openly admired her broad, fresh-scrubbed face and long, clean hair. She was so good, his Leah, wanting nothing more than to please him. He didn't deserve her.

"What time's your meeting?" Jared asked.

"Starts at 7:00 p.m., but I'm going early to help set up. It will only take me a few minutes to get there. And it's *our* meeting," she added, mildly nagging, "It's your church, too."

She looked up into Jared's face, "I know they'd love it if you could be there."

"I already promised Howard and Matt I'd go to the game, hon," Jared said, smiling down at her, unfazed.

Leah gave in, "Well, I know it's important for men to do guy things. I just wish you could come. I know you'd enjoy it."

"I promise I'll go next time."

He gave her a tender kiss on the cheek, "Don't wait up for us, we won't be home until late—double header and Howard's treating for dinner."

"Okay, I'll take notes," hesitating briefly before adding, "The missionaries from Africa are speaking tonight."

"Sure, sounds good," Jared answered.

Holding Leah by both arms, he pulled her in for a more substantial, reassuring kiss, which made her weak in the knees.

"We're going to have to get married soon . . . ," he murmured in her ear.

Blushing, she fumbled for her keys and opened the car door.

"Let's get this show on the road!" Howard's voice boomed as he clattered down the wooden stairs from his office.

Elizabeth, who was finishing a piece in the practice area, waved them off, smiling briefly at Howard before turning her concentration back to her work.

Matt emerged from somewhere, ignoring both Elizabeth and Leah as he strode past.

Matt and Howard got into Howard's GL 450, while Jared tucked Leah into their beat-up, brown Corolla, bestowing an additional kiss on her forehead for the road, with another promise to go with her next time.

Howard revved the engine to hurry him along, the Quakes game started in less than an hour.

49

Most Saturday nights the Church of the Living Christ was full, but tonight it was packed. Tonight was a double header: missionary night and youth basketball.

Of the three missionary couples scheduled to speak, only the Carters of the Ghana mission had shown up, so he was able to use the full version of his PowerPoint instead of the abbreviated one he had prepared. The couple was still answering questions at 7:45 p.m., when the pastor stood up to give the benediction. Youth basketball started promptly at 8:00 p.m. and his son was the star forward.

During their presentation, Leah sat mesmerized. She yearned to be like the Carters. Mr. Carter, cheerfully rotund and ruddy-cheeked, full of the Spirit. Mrs. Carter, replete in her boxy, blue suit, nude nylons, and matching, flex-soled pumps. Leah thought her perfect in every way.

Several times during the presentation Mr. Carter praised his wife's unflagging support, without which, he insisted, none of his work could have been accomplished.

At one point, his voice filled with emotion and his eyes with tears, he shared, "When the man follows Christ, and the woman follows the man, all is as it should be in God's kingdom, and the Lord's work will be done! Things must be done the Lord's way!"

The Carters were middle-aged, their family grown, but there had been families with young children at the mission as well. In fact, young families were needed, he said, particularly those who could teach youth a trade. Seeing a young American family live righteously was better than the most powerful sermon, he said, to convert these people to the Gospel. If any young couples were interested, they were to contact their local pastor for further information on how to proceed.

Increasingly excited, Leah took careful notes, including the Carters' address in Ghana, to which they were returning next month. The pastor was hustling everyone out, but she caught up to them in the parking lot to ask a few more questions and see how she and Jared might fit in.

They were delighted to speak with her. She told them Jared was a glassblower, but they were both young and strong, willing to do any work. She was thrilled when they said that Jared's skill was one they could use at their mission.

Glassblowing technicians were needed in a factory in the Greater Accra region. And they didn't waste their time making useless fruit bowls and flower vases for the rich, but useful, glass tubing for industry.

The Carters had been looking for a way to keep young men in the area. Jared could train them with basic glassblowing skills, Leah could teach them English, and the Carters said the church would front the expense of setting up a small glassblowing facility—nothing fancy, but good enough, and they could have a small house to live in, also. They would, of course, have to get married first. She assured them they were engaged, not just boyfriend and girlfriend. She also made sure they knew they slept separately, that they were not living in sin.

She couldn't wait to share the news with Jared tomorrow. What a perfect opportunity for them! Maybe they could go right away, starting their new lives as missionaries while they started their new family. And if Jared still wanted to do bowls and other art pieces, there were always people with money to spend in any country. That would be okay, because they could donate the money to the Church! Jared would be happy, and his work would be contributing to good in the world.

Driving back to the compound, Leah allowed herself to feel the first glimmer of peace. Maybe she had finally worked hard enough, done enough good, to merit the Lord's forgiveness. In Africa, she could leave her past behind and start her new life with Jared. That must be the Lord's plan. Why else would He put this great opportunity in their path?

In the morning, she'd introduce Jared to the Carters at church.

50

Cushioned as she was by the spiritual glow enveloping her, Leah entered and left the quad without noticing Elizabeth's lack of greeting. After floating up the stairs, her mind full of plans for her and Jared, she fished in her purse for her keys. She saw the warped flooring and the splintery, plywood door. Now that she'd made up her mind, she couldn't wait to get away.

Energized and lifted, she unlocked her door, put her purse down on the small table to her left. The only other furniture in the room—a narrow, twin bed—took up the entire wall opposite the door.

She began getting ready for bed. Reaching into the small closet to the right, at the foot of the bed, she lifted her pajamas off the hook from the back of the door. It had taken her a while to find something thick enough and with long sleeves. Anything in the women's department was usually inappropriate—too tight, too low, or just too flimsy. You could see right through most of them.

She finally found this pair in the men's department at Goodwill. They were comfortable and modest, so she could walk back and forth from her room to the bathroom and not worry if she bumped into anyone on the way.

After changing, she hung her jumper and t-shirt up on a wire hanger next to several more t-shirts and her overalls. Although her work clothes were changed daily, she could wear the jumper for church several times before having to wash it.

Next, looking for her shower slippers, she lifted the chenille bedspread, pushing aside a plastic storage container to get at them. Before she pushed the storage container back in, she took some time to touch each item in it. This small ritual calmed her.

First in the long, flat box was a large skein of silky wool yarn, the pretty color of new green leaves. Next was a child's toy, a handcrafted set of pick-up sticks. Two expensive-looking obsidian knives with bone handles, each about four inches long, gleamed incongruously next to a cheap, metal napkin dispenser, the kind you see in old-fashioned diners. Scarves and other trinkets, everything from jewelry to old cell phones and pens, filled the spaces. Satisfied, she pushed the box back under the bed and pulled the spread back down, smoothing it until it hung straight and covered her small treasures.

Gathering her toothbrush, toothpaste and a washcloth, she went back out into the hall and walked down the stairs toward the bathroom she and Elizabeth shared. The men used the one at the other end.

When she got there, Leah was irritated to find Elizabeth already occupying it. Reflexively, she glanced at the quad. Elizabeth must have finished her piece and placed it in the annealing oven, or she was taking a break. Hesitating briefly, but needing to pee as well as brush her teeth and wash her face, Leah knocked. Two short raps. Just enough to let her know she was waiting, but not enough to be demanding. She hoped. She didn't like making people mad, especially Elizabeth or Matt.

No response.

Feeling angry, but unwilling to knock again, Leah folded her arms and stuck one leg out stubbornly, to wait. She couldn't hear the shower running. How long could it take to go to the bathroom?

Several long minutes later, Elizabeth emerged, brushing by Leah as if she weren't there. Leah was used to being ignored, but was surprised Elizabeth hadn't made a snide comment or complained about the knock.

Once inside, Leah locked the door. Setting her toothbrush on a clean paper towel on the Formica counter next to the stainless steel sink, she let the water run hot, backed it off a bit, then squirted soap from the dispenser on her wash rag and began scrubbing her face. It was perfectly good soap. She had never seen any reason to buy special soap for her face. That was all a marketing ploy. She rinsed thoroughly, squeezed the washrag almost dry, then laid it, neatly folded, to the side. Next, she squeezed Colgate onto her toothbrush, ran it under the water once, and began cleaning her teeth, counting to herself.

"Ten, nine, eight . . . " in each section, careful to brush down only, not sideways. Rinse, pat face dry. Cleanliness was next to godliness.

Wiping her damp hands on her pajama bottoms, leaving the toothbrush to dry on the sink for a minute, she turned to use the toilet. When she was finished, she pulled up her pants and turned to flush. Something in the small wastebasket next to the toilet caught her eye.

Something like a small, white thermometer was partially sticking up out of the trash. Was Elizabeth sick?

Curious, Leah got a fresh paper towel, reached down and lifted it out. Squinting, holding it up to the fluorescent light over the sink so she could see better, she rotated it a quarter turn. There, in the center of a small circle, were two, distinct, vertical, pink lines. One light, one dark. Even Leah knew what those pink lines meant.

Her breath caught, time telescoped.

All those nights she and Jared worked together, all of Jared's innocent help had been twisted and taken advantage of by that woman! *Her* Jared, *her* man!

It wasn't his fault, she knew. She had denied him. He had wanted to become intimate, to do 'it', but she had refused him, telling him they had to wait until they got married.

She should have known. Men were weak creatures, she understood this. Even Jared was apparently not immune. They needed a virtuous woman.

Maybe she could still help him.

51

It took a minute for Leah to collect herself and, by the time she did, her anger was full force—directed not at Jared, but exclusively and completely at Elizabeth.

With the strength of the righteous, she marched into the quad to confront her rival, only to find she'd already left. She checked her room, but she either wasn't there, or wasn't answering.

Typical. She just breezes in and out, destroying lives.

Robbed of the satisfaction of an immediate, self-righteous confrontation, Leah's mood plummeted. She robotically walked back up the stairs to her room, changed into the work clothes she planned on wearing the next day and, although it was 9:00 p.m. at night, began to load up her backpack for work. She reached under the bed and, after admiring them again, touched each item in the box for comfort.

She selected one of the obsidian knives, the skein of luxurious wool yarn and the wooden toy. She couldn't bring herself to return everything yet, but she'd start with these—and maybe the Lord would forgive her. Maybe it was her own lack of purity that had caused this. If she returned the stolen items, maybe God would take this pain away, remove this obstacle from their path. Her and Jared's path to Africa.

She could return the items to the various vendor booths before anyone else got there. She knew it was wrong to steal, but just couldn't stop herself sometimes. She would be walking somewhere, and when she got home, a new item would be in her bag.

Her next stop was the kitchenette downstairs, which consisted of little more than a two-burner stove, a large, double stainless steel sink, and a small refrigerator. She completed her morning routine, filling a five-gallon jug with filtered water and fresh lemon slices. She made sure Jared always had a fresh one inside the cage. Although originally intended only for Jared, there was no way to keep the other glassblowers from enjoying the refreshing water, too. She hoisted it into her car by its nylon handle and drove to the festival.

Tonight, all astral objects remained safely in their respective places in the sky, a safe distance from each other, but the cosmos had other plans for Leah and Elizabeth.

Barely aware of her surroundings, her mind going over which objects to return first after delivering the water jug, Leah let herself in the back gate with her set of keys. Howard gave them each one for the duration of the festival. Hooking her thumb under the strap, she hoisted up the heavy jug onto her right shoulder, transferring the pack to her left hand to balance the weight.

Leah successfully returned the skein of yarn on the way to the glassblower's demo cage. She could hear the roar of the furnace even before she came around the corner.

She hadn't expected to see anyone down here at night.

SHATTERED

Elizabeth, dripping in sweat, feet planted squarely in front of the glory hole, was dancing with fire. Sinewy arm muscles working efficiently, entirely focused on the metal pole she was dipping into the pool of fiery-hot, molten glass, she neither saw nor heard her enemy.

Keeping her eyes on Elizabeth, Leah slowly opened the wire gate, sat the glass jug on the inside of the door as always, then stood there, backpack still in hand, at a loss for words. All the powerful accusations that arose in her mind upon discovering the pregnancy test escaped her now.

She could only blurt out, "What are you doing here?"

Elizabeth glanced back, but kept on working.

"Go away."

"Do not ignore me!" Leah said.

She was so tired of being treated like a nobody, the nobody who fetched and carried and cleaned up after everyone. Elizabeth didn't even apologize! It was as if she didn't count, like she wasn't even a person! She was Jared's fiancé! Elizabeth had no right to seduce him. She just took whatever she wanted— everything important, beautiful, and clean. She just stomped it into the ground, then acted as if nothing happened. Elizabeth was carrying *her* baby, the one she and Jared were supposed to raise and nurture in the Gospel. This baby was *hers*, not Elizabeth's!

Rooted to the spot, backpack still on her shoulder, fists clenched at her sides, all she could do was impotently repeat herself, louder this time.

"I will *not* go away!"

With resigned patience, as if dealing with a stray dog that kept bugging her for scraps, Elizabeth wiped sweat off her forehead with the back of a terry-cloth wristband.

"Look, I don't know why you followed me down here, and I don't know why you're still here, but I need to work right now."

"Alone," she said, turning back to her work. "Nothing personal."

52

*N**othing personal??*

Leah bubbled with rage.

She was being dismissed again! Elizabeth didn't even give her a chance to confront her with what she had done, without some explanation of why she shattered someone else's life without a second thought.

Leah stood there, staring at Elizabeth as she continued to ignore her.

The moon watched Leah.

Something clicked. Without thinking, Leah calmly picked up her loaded backpack and fueled with a growing rage she had never felt before, swung it directly at the back of Elizabeth's head. The rail-thin glassblower crumpled beneath the blow.

"*That's* personal, whore!" Leah cried, shaking all over.

Grabbing the obsidian knife from her backpack, Leah let loose, stabbing again and again.

Then, just as quickly as the fury had struck, it left. Oblivious to the bloody wreck lying next to her, Leah sat back on her heels and wiped the obsidian blade clean on the bib of her overalls—the picture of calm.

Checking it for any remaining blood, she noticed a small piece of the tip had broken off. She couldn't return it to Thomas and Lisa's booth now. And she didn't want to take it home. She looked around for ideas, then smiled.

Walking over to the open glass furnace, she tossed the knife into the glory hole.

"Dust to dust . . . or glass to glass, in this case," she chuckled, giddy at the easy vanquishing of her enemy, and her clever disposal of the murder weapon. God had indeed been good. He used even her weakness to deliver her enemy unto her, and the means of eliminating her.

She needed to clean this mess up, then go home and shower. She'd have to throw away her clothes. That was okay. She wore the same work clothes every day. No one would notice. The guys would still be at the game, and Elizabeth wouldn't be there to tell on her, would she?

She knelt down then and, just to be sure, rested her fingers gently on the side of the young woman's damp neck. Nothing. Good.

She looked down at her. Funny how she didn't take up much space. Just a moment ago, Elizabeth had filled the cage with her power. She had the kind of energy no one could ignore. She always made Leah feel as if there wasn't enough air to breathe when they were in the same room.

Leah sat back down on her heels, arms resting on her knees, allowing herself to savor her victory for another minute, and stared up at the dark sky. Stars glimmered and the moon shone low on the horizon. A Great-Horned Owl announced the hour. God must be pleased.

He had sanctioned murder plenty of times in the Bible. The Canaanites, men, women, and children, the guy who tried to steady the ark, even Isaac, Abraham's beloved son. For righteous purposes only, of course, and what more righteous purpose was there, than saving her Jared from a whore of Babylon? The good she and Jared would do in Africa more than outweighed the loss of one, wicked life. That's how God worked in the Old Testament. Why not now?

She sat like that for another few minutes, making sure no pulse remained.

Finally, she stood up and stretched, her surroundings coming into focus, thinking about what needed to be done.

Matt opened tomorrow. She remembered the argument between him and Elizabeth in the break area a week or so ago. Yes, that would work nicely. Matt needed to be punished.

Elizabeth weighed less than the bags of sand Leah regularly hauled around, so lifting her into the annealing oven was easy. She had the extra satisfaction of breaking several of Matt's larger pieces in the process, as she bent and pushed the body in, making it fit.

Hosing off the cement took only another twenty minutes. It was strangely relaxing. She'd be home and tucked into bed by 10:30 p.m., 11:00 p.m. at the latest. She hoisted her backpack onto her shoulder.

After killing someone, returning stolen items to their rightful owners didn't seem like such a high priority.

53

FRIDAY, JUNE 21

True to his profession, if not his word, the contractor was two hours late. Logan was having him install some storage cabinets and shelves in the back corner, next to the washer and dryer. She wanted lunch about an hour ago, so was grumpy when he finally arrived.

Quickly walking with him out to the garage, she planned on making sure he knew where she wanted everything, then going to get something to eat. When she opened the small side door, which she hadn't bothered getting a lock for yet, she looked down and saw something sticking out on the other side of her new washer and dryer, right where her new shelves were going to go.

Looking over her shoulder, Bill, according to his nametag, said, "Looks like somebody's been making themselves at home."

They walked in farther and saw a pile of blankets and a pillow tucked underneath the sagging, wooden workbench along the back wall of the garage. The blankets had been straightened, and there was no trash littering the floor. At least her squatter was neat.

"We get some homeless people down here at the beach," Bill said. "Most of them are harmless, you just have to lock things up," he said, implying she should have known that and was somehow responsible for someone camping out in her garage.

Maybe he was right, but it gave her an unsettled feeling to know some unknown person had been sleeping in her garage, just a few feet from the house. She wondered if they let themselves in the other night, and that's why her doors were open when she came home. If so, apparently she had nothing worth stealing.

She shook it off. Whatever the reason, whoever it was, she'd solve the problem by locking the door next time. Not knowing who to give them back to, they threw the blankets and pillow in the trash, in case they had creepy crawlies. She wished she could give them back to whatever homeless person brought them, so they'd be warm at least, wherever they found a place to sleep.

The maternal part of her rose in her chest, but she beat it back down, knowing she could not save the world. She'd have to ask around and see if there was a shelter she could donate to. She was vaguely aware that back in the '80s, California dumped thousands of mentally ill patients onto the street to save the state money. Not everyone was on the street through some fault of his or her own.

Satisfied the contractor didn't need her after he got started, lunch called and she walked down to Tava'e's, promising to be back in plenty of time to pay him. He said he should be done in a couple hours.

From the limited lunch menu, Logan selected a large, *Nicoise* salad with a generous slice of fresh-out-of-the-oven

French bread. After polishing off her meal, she went back up to the counter and ordered a tall iced coffee to go.

She was just replacing the lid after stirring in two sugars when the saloon doors from the kitchen swung open, expelling a young man with familiar features. It took her a minute, but then his face came together all at once and she recognized him. The jaw line was more pronounced, and he had less baby fat and was taller, but it was Danny, all grown up.

If it took her a few minutes to recognize him, he had no such hesitation, "Hello Music Lady!" he sang out cheerfully.

He held a large tray of croissants Epiphany helped him unload into the case. From the way she spoke to him, touching him gently on the arm, and the myriad signals they were giving off, she could tell they were an item.

How about that.

Danny had somehow not only gotten himself out of jail, but got himself a girlfriend, too!

He had gone back through the swinging doors into the kitchen after unloading his tray, unencumbered by the normal social obligation of coming over to talk to Logan.

Epiphany did walk over, with a shrug and a shy smile.

"Hi, Logan. I wanted to explain about Danny staying in your garage. It was my idea. He needed someplace safe during the day, until I could figure something out. When I told Tava'e, she said she'd help. He's staying at their place for a while."

She went to take someone's order before Logan could think of an appropriate response. At least the mystery squatter situation had been explained.

Later, Epiphany filled her in with the rest of the story. Logan learned that for lack of evidence, the Portland police weren't going to pursue the case against Danny. The video from the security camera was old, and the only bit that actually recorded showed only the other boy, James, who initiated the robbery. Since Danny had no previous criminal record or history of violence, they let him go.

His mother, Neva, was beside herself that her boy was safe and could come home, but his father was not so forgiving. He made it clear Danny was no longer welcome. He had accepted the reality of Danny's mental challenges when he was a child, but having a "grown idiot around the house forever" was not something he was willing to tolerate.

Epiphany had known Danny when they were in high school, both of them being outcasts. She saw him sitting on the beach with nowhere to go after he got off the bus James had given him the money for in Portland. She made the plan to hide Danny out in Logan's garage. She knew the contractors were working on the main house, but nobody was bothering with the garage. He stayed in his mom's booth at night, at least he did until he was discovered and arrested. Prior to that, when the festival opened, he had just blended in with the crowds and Epiphany gave him a ride to his daytime hideout every morning before work. She took him back there temporarily, even after his release from jail, until she went to Tava'e for help. She had intended to go back to remove the blankets that night, but Logan and the contractor had discovered the bed before she could get off work.

Tava'e and Jean took Danny on as an apprentice baker, since he knew a little already, and loved the work. It was an easy next step to give him a room in their home. According to Epiphany, he wasn't the first young person they had taken in. Tava'e's heart was as large as she was.

54

The contractor finished early and left his bill in an envelope taped to the outside of the new garage door.

Trusting soul.

Taking the bill off the door, Logan went inside to try to reach Lisa again. She picked up on the first ring, as if she had been waiting by the phone, which she had.

"Logan?"

"Hey, I was just calling to check in. I tried to call earlier, but you didn't answer," Logan said, "You okay?"

"No, I'm not all right. Do you have a minute to talk?"

"Of course," Logan said.

"I went to see Detective Andrews today."

So that's where she'd been.

Before Logan could object, she continued," I know what you said, but I couldn't wait any more, knowing Thomas was in jail because of me."

"I thought the investigator was going to call with good news? It sounded like that was a done deal," Logan said.

"Well, I haven't heard from him," Lisa said, "And I decided it didn't matter anyway. I just wanted to get this cleared up. Get Thomas out of jail. I told him everything about me and my involvement with *The Way*. About the investigator we hired to clear my name and set things right for that man's daughter.

"What did he say? Is Thomas out? Is he home, now?" Logan asked.

"He didn't care! He just said that was an FBI matter and had nothing to do with the case against Thomas! Even after I explained that Thomas knew I was either going to clear my name or turn myself in, pointing out that it removed all doubt of Thomas having any motive to stop Elizabeth from blackmailing us again, which he said she probably would have continued to do, having gotten eight-thousand dollars out of him so easily the first time. He just said that didn't mean anything. None of it! He said all the evidence still pointed to Thomas, and that he was staying right where he was. In fact, they were charging him with first-degree murder, no bail!

"This is like some nightmare that won't end. Nothing I could say moved him, even though it is so obvious Thomas didn't do anything, he definitely wouldn't murder anyone. He's never even been in a fight that I know of. Now, me, on the other hand . . . "

Logan let her get it all out. Lisa talked for another ten minutes straight, telling and retelling the conversation from various angles.

When she finally wound down, Logan asked her a few clarifying questions to make sure she understood, then told Lisa she would come over the next day so they could brainstorm solutions. Nothing they could do this late.

"Have you eaten?" Logan asked.

"Not yet," Lisa admitted. "I keep trying to get a hold of the investigator, but so far no luck."

"Well, maybe he's out on another case. I know it's frustrating, but he'll probably call you tonight or tomorrow. For now, get yourself some dinner, take a long, hot bath, and go to bed early. Doctor Logan's orders," she said. "Things always look better in the morning."

Logan didn't really think so. There was no way a murder charge would look any better in the morning, but their brains would be fresher and they'd come up with some plan to help Thomas or at least to make sure Lisa didn't crack under the strain in the meantime.

Two hours later, her cell rang. It was Lisa. Her speech was slurred and Logan could barely hear her.

"So sorry to bother you, again, Logan . . . think I need to go to the hospital. Heart feels funny, can't stand . . . dizzy . . . "

Then silence.

"Don't move! On my way!" Logan shouted into the phone.

Logan dialed 911, but beat the ambulance there and took Lisa to the hospital. Lisa could walk, but just barely.

*****

It was three in the morning before Logan got back home, so tired she could hardly move herself. The ER had been backed up, as usual, on a Friday night, but they'd finally gotten Lisa admitted. She looked only gray instead of white as she had when they first arrived, so the admitting nurse made her wait. Apparently, you had to be dead already in order to be seen in less than an hour.

The chairs were hard, the magazines old and sticky, and if she hadn't been so worried about Lisa, she would have been afraid to breathe the air.

When she finally left, Lisa was sleeping peacefully, floating on some cocktail of drugs Logan wished she had right now, hooked up to several machines monitoring her vital signs. The doctor said it was a good thing she brought her in when she did—another hour and she probably would have suffered irreparable damage—she'd had a stroke.

Exhausted, Logan dropped into bed still semi-dressed, knowing she'd have to get up and go see Thomas in the morning.

She was up again in thirty minutes, too tired to sleep. Dimebox, always a night owl, kept her company as she shuffled down the stairs and went into the kitchen to make some herbal tea Glenda had given her. Feeling a sore throat coming on, she added a slice of lemon to the cup before pouring in the steaming hot water over the stainless steel loose-leaf tea holder. Glenda had included it with her purchase, saying tea bags weren't real tea. The good stuff came loose leaf.

Breathing in the jasmine-scented steam immediately began to loosen her tight neck muscles. Curled up on the couch with Dimebox, she allowed her eyelids to get heavy and her mind to drift, reviewing the case against Thomas, Lisa's worsening illness and troubled past. Their problems were mounting, increasingly beyond her meager skills. Nancy Drew she was not.

At least there was *some* good news. Danny was out of jail and landed among friends at Tava'e's.

Tea finished and too tired to drag herself up the stairs to bed, with her last ounce of energy she pushed the pillow she'd had at her lower back up to the end of the couch. Fluffing it up, she lay down, letting her head sink gratefully onto the soft cushion.

Just for a minute . . .

55

The sun streamed in the kitchen window and Dimebox was mewing for his breakfast. He'd been out all night and probably fed by half the neighborhood already, but he still expected his morning meal.

Sandy-eyed and stiff, Logan instantly regretted not having hauled herself to bed the night before, no matter how tired she was. Sleeping in your clothes was not recommended. She felt sticky and yearned for a hot shower.

Feeding Dimebox first, putting on a pot of coffee, Logan made her way upstairs and into the shower, grateful all over again for excellent water pressure and the shower-head she had raised when they did the remodel. Washing her hair, scrubbing herself awake, she allowed herself to think of nothing but the wonderful hot water pounding on her head.

Much better!

Dressing quickly, knowing she couldn't put off talking to Thomas, she went downstairs to find her cell, which was still in her purse on the coffee table.

Seeing her teacup from the night before, she took it into the kitchen and tapped it gently on the side of the trashcan to unglued the lemon slice where it had adhered to the side. It didn't look like Ben was home, so Logan went back in the living room, dug her phone out of her purse and plopped down on the couch. Dimebox immediately jumped up to claim her lap.

As she absentmindedly pet him, something niggled at the back of her brain, but it would have to wait until after she talked with Thomas, if she could even get through to him. She didn't know if he'd be less available now that he'd been charged with murder. It made you realize how little you know about the legal system until someone you cared about was caught in its tangles.

She still couldn't believe any of this was happening.

One of the women on duty knew Rick and got Thomas on the phone fairly quickly. When he answered she summarized what had happened to Lisa, downplaying it as much as possible so as not to worry him more than necessary.

"They're just keeping her for observation, really. She was resting peacefully when I left—sound asleep."

When Thomas spoke, it was devoid of his usual, relaxed confidence.

"I want you to know I appreciate all you've done already. I hate to ask you for more help, but I can't be there, so . . . if you don't mind looking in on her . . . "

"Of course, you idiot—what do you think I'd do? I'm off for the summer, remember? Teachers have these long vacations. We just sit around and eat bon-bons. Completely overpaid, right? Your nephews have the booth covered and Sally's back playing with Ned several nights a week, so I have almost nothing to do. Keeping an eye on Lisa is an easy thing. I don't want you to worry about that. She'll be fine."

"Okay. Thanks," Thomas said, sounding tired.

Getting back to her friend's more urgent problem, she gathered her courage and asked about the murder charge. Facing things directly was always best, Logan thought, like pulling a Band-Aid off quick.

"What happens next? Do you have an attorney? Do you want me to find someone for you?"

As if she knew anyone.

"No, Dad takes care of Henderson's cars. He's that lawyer in LA who has a place down here on the beach. Not sure how I'm going to pay him, but Dad says he's good. Dad has the money. Says he never spends any of it and never goes anywhere, but if he does hire him, I'll pay him back. I'm sorry I didn't tell you everything. I just thought everything would be okay—that it wouldn't get this far."

"It's okay, Thomas. Lisa explained most of it. Have you seen him yet, the lawyer?"

"Only talked to him on the phone. He's coming down today."

"I know this isn't exactly like getting in trouble for smoking under the bleachers," reminding him of the time his smoking got them both Saturday detention, "but it will work out."

It has to.

Thomas also gave her the name and number of the investigator.

"Maybe if that is settled, Lisa will have one less thing to worry about, besides me, and that will help. Her lupus flares up when she's stressed. I've got to get her to her aunt's. She needs that healing ceremony. I'm not sure I believe in it, but she does, and that's all that matters."

Logan agreed.

Nothing else to say, she promised to take care of Lisa and call the investigator, and he promised to keep her posted, as often as he could, about what the lawyer had to say after they met, although he didn't sound hopeful.

Thomas dismally reported that at the arraignment, Detective Andrews told the judge he was certain Thomas clearly had motive, means, and opportunity. Blackmail was the motive, and since he was the only one who made obsidian knives, he had the means. As for opportunity, he'd been seen at the festival that morning, within the time frame the ME had established as the time of Elizabeth's death.

The case looked pretty airtight.

Logan knew he didn't do it. She went over everything she could think of, everything she had learned, as she cleaned up the kitchen after they got off the phone. There had to be something, some small detail that would at least give her a clue as to where to start proving Thomas' innocence.

As she was emptying the trash, something caught her eye. A thin, yellow something.

Leah always brought a jug of water every morning for Jared. She put it just inside the door of the glassblower's demonstration cage.

Logan could clearly see it as it looked that morning, when she snuck in to see what was going on, sparkling in the sun, with bright yellow, lemon slices floating in it, a silent witness to the hurried comings and goings of the crime scene team, the morning Matt discovered Elizabeth's body.

If the water jug was there, that meant Leah must have been there before Matt arrived. She may have seen something or someone, some clue that would break the case.

Why hadn't she come forward? Had she seen Elizabeth's dead body and been frightened into silence? Or had she seen the killer? Maybe it was left over from the day before. Well, she wouldn't know unless she asked.

56

Deciphering her scribbles took a minute, but after one misread number, Logan managed to dial correctly and get in touch with one Mr. Woodrow, the investigator digging for information to clear Lisa's name and set things up for a scholarship for the Bureau of Indian Affairs man's high-school daughter. He picked up just as she was preparing to leave a message.

"Hello?"

"Mr. Woodrow?"

"Yes?"

"Mr. Woodrow, my name is Logan McKenna. I'm a friend of Thomas and Lisa Delgado. I don't know if you've heard about the recent trouble, but neither of them can meet with you right now, so they've asked me to contact you and find out what's happening on your end. How is the investigation coming? I'd love to have good news to share with them. They could use it."

The investigator, who knew most of what had happened with Thomas, but not that Lisa's lupus had flared up and put her in the hospital, said he needed to verify who she was. Apparently having done so successfully, he called her back within the hour and proceeded to give her a full report.

She took notes as fast as she could write before he informed her a formal, written report was in the mail to Thomas and Lisa, along with instructions for setting up the scholarship. He had been very successful on both clearing Lisa's name and structuring a scholarship in such a way the young woman would be able to attend just about any good university of her choice, barring the ivy leagues, and never know who her benefactors were.

The FBI it turned out, had never put Lisa on a most-wanted list. They'd been watching the group for about eight months prior to the bombing, and knew all about the increasingly radical leader, and that she had left him months before the incident resulting in the Indian agent's death.

All the years she'd been hiding her true identity had been unnecessary, but there had been no way for her to know. Logan let this sink in. Lisa's infant daughter may have lived had she not had to hide her with her relatives on the reservation, where she later contracted meningitis. There was no way to go back in time and undo decisions made. She wondered if Lisa would grieve all over again for her baby daughter, or eventually gain peace, knowing there was no way to know how things would have worked out had she taken a different path.

We have so little control sometimes, she thought, before calling Thomas at the jail to deliver the news that at least he did not have to worry about Lisa being arrested by the FBI. They would not bring him to the phone this time, so she left a cryptic message—Lisa okay, all clear—and asked him to call when he could.

Next stop, the hospital, to share the bittersweet news.

After fueling Lola and making two more phone calls, one to Ben and one to Rick, she finally made it to the hospital.

SHATTERED

She arrived at dinner time to find a much improved, if still pale, Lisa, sitting up in bed, black hair fanned across the white pillow behind her. Her arms rested on a slim shelf table, topped by a tray of unidentifiable, beige food. The only bright spot was a square of red Jello.

"Not exactly *posole* and fry bread, is it?" Logan said in greeting. "I'll have to bring you something edible next time I come."

"Please do! Fire Fries with extra sauce, preferably," Lisa replied, "just don't try to make fry bread!"

She moved the tray aside, patting the bed next to her.

"You said you had some good news. Tell me everything!" she said, her eyes shining with hope.

Her speech was much improved, but Logan noticed she helped her left arm with her right when she moved the tray.

Logan did her best to give her Woodrow's whole report, but assured her that a complete, written version was on its way, so she could go over it in detail at her leisure.

The nurse popped her head in the door, warning Logan to keep her visit short, as Lisa needed to conserve her energy. According to her doctor, she had only suffered a Transient Ischemic Attack, a mini-stroke, but needed to make sure she didn't overexert or become too excited, or she could suffer from a full-blown stroke, which could result in permanent paralysis or even death.

If Lisa's thoughts ran to the what-ifs or regrets surrounding her years of hiding and her decision to leave her infant daughter with her mother on the reservation, she did not say. She exhibited a new aura of calm and acceptance Logan attributed to Lisa's aunt, who had flown in that afternoon and had just gone down to the cafeteria to try to find something healthier for her favorite niece to eat. This was the Native American healer who was going to have the balancing ceremony for her back in Idaho when she was well enough to travel.

"Aunt Margaret and I had a long talk. I feel free. Maybe that's what happens when you give up trying to control things you never had power over in the first place. Even before you brought me the good news, I knew things would be okay."

She sighed and leaned back against the pillows leaning on the wall, "Now we just have to free Thomas."

"I'm afraid you need to leave now, Ma'am," the nurse said, more firmly this time, leaning in to interrupt their conversation. "Visiting hours are over. You can come back tomorrow after 10:00 a.m."

Unwilling to burden her friend with unwarranted hope or point the finger of blame, however inadvertently, at another, probably innocent person, Logan did not share her observation with Lisa about Leah possibly being at the festival early that morning. She decided to wait until she had a chance to talk with Jared's girlfriend in person. She needed to find out why she had been there, and what she may have seen.

Too many people jumped to conclusions, including Detective Andrews. He cobbled together convenient facts to get the job done, first pointing the finger at Thomas, then at Danny, then back at Thomas again. The facts did point to Thomas, but since she knew Thomas must be innocent, she felt Andrews should have done a more careful job.

It's possible Leah saw Matt and Elizabeth in an argument that turned deadly. If Matt knew Leah had witnessed the murder . . . she needed to convince the young woman to go to the police immediately . . . for her own protection.

It was too late tonight, but first thing in the morning, she planned to drive out to the school and talk with the young maker of heart-shaped glass paperweights and pusher of religious pamphlets.

57

Lola was running a little rough. She'd have to take her into Mr. Delgado as soon as she got some time. She checked her watch. The glassblowers' school was only a mile up the road, and not much out of her way. She could drive by and if the lights were on, see if Leah was up.

Lights were not only on, but both front doors stood wide open, throwing the shrubs around the front stairs into stark relief. She pulled up in front and turned off the engine. Lola pinged a few times, then quieted down. She could see a silhouette of Howard through his office window and someone working at the furnace. They must not keep regular hours. A symphony of crickets filled the soft, night air.

Feeling foolish already, she started to turn around and go home. It was late and her imagination was probably working overtime. Lemon slices, really? That was her big clue?

Before she could turn around, Howard caught sight of her and waved.

Shit. Might as well get this over with.

Leah was the only person she hadn't talked to yet, but it was doubtful she knew anything. Logan didn't mind embarrassing herself for Thomas, but once this was over, she was going to keep her nose out of it. Thomas had an attorney now. A high-powered one who probably had a team of investigators—any of whom were more qualified than her. Starting tomorrow, she would focus on being there for Lisa.

Waving back to Howard, she mounted the stairs and looked around for Leah.

Matt was the one working at the furnace. In spite of her mission, she couldn't help but watch for a few minutes. At the moment, he was opening up the neck of a large, deep-red vase with what looked like a giant pair of tweezers she heard the glassblowers refer to as "jacks." Not wanting to interrupt him at work, she turned left and knocked on Howard's open office door.

"Hi, come on in," Howard waved her in, getting up from behind his desk, taking off a pair of black-framed reading glasses. "Just sorting through some paperwork, it tends to outrun me these days."

She came up with a story about stopping by to see Leah for a few minutes, hoping to get the name of her and Jared's church. New to the area, wanted to make new friends, that sort of thing. Leah had given her a pamphlet.

It was frightening how good she was getting at lying. Well, it had always been a gift.

Howard pointed to the first door at the top of the stairs.

"That's Leah's room. Her door's open and the light's on, so I'm sure it's okay if you go on up. Good thing you stopped by tonight, she and Jared are leaving in the morning for Helsinki."

She must have looked at him blankly, because he added, "The contest . . . you know. Jared's going now that Elizabeth is gone."

How many euphemisms were there for the word 'dead'?

Artificially brightening his voice, he continued, "Jared should be back soon, he had to go up to LA to straighten out a problem with his visa. They thought his name was the same as someone on the no-fly list. Leah got hers yesterday, but they wouldn't give him his. He had to go back up today. Nightmare dealing with things like this ever since 9/11."

"Do you need a visa just to visit Finland for a few days?" Logan asked.

"No, but they're going to Africa directly from there. They were offered some kind of missionary assignment in Ghana through Leah's church, and plan on staying there more than three months. That's the limit they give you, otherwise you have to fly out and fly back in again, which would be prohibitively expensive."

"Don't they need shots and things?" the mother in Logan asked, remembering Amy's malaria pills and series of immunizations.

"That's what I thought, but they're young and think they're invincible. Jared said they're going to get them there, it's cheaper."

They talked for a few more minutes before Logan excused herself. She had to cross the quad to get to the stairs that lead up to Leah's room.

Having tapped his piece free from the metal pole, he was placing it in the annealing oven. She wondered if thoughts of Elizabeth even crossed his mind. He either didn't see her or chose to ignore her, congruent with his sparkling personality.

Keeping the metal railing on her right for safety, but not using it for support, she focused instead on using her stomach and leg muscles as she mounted the stairs toward Leah's room. The physical therapist said taking the stairs were good for her and would strengthen her lower back, as long as she did it correctly. Who knew she'd been doing everything wrong all these years, including opening drawers, walking up stairs, and reaching for things in the back seat.

Leah's door was half-open, creating a long, yellow triangle of light across an otherwise dark floor. Sounds of metal scraping on metal, probably hangers on a closet rod, let her know Leah was home.

Logan's knock brought Leah, hanger in hand, to the door. Before she opened it, she quickly kicked a low, flat container back under the bed, but not before Logan saw a bundle of pick-up sticks she'd seen in the toymaker's booth at the festival and what looked like a bone handle of some kind. Was that one of Thomas' knives? If she bought them, why was she hiding them?

58

Leah glared at her visitor.

"What are you doing here?"

"I'm sorry to bother you. Howard said it was okay to come up," Logan replied, attempting a nonchalant tone, "I was driving back from visiting a friend in the hospital and decided to stop by on my way home to see if you were up. Tomorrow is Sunday and I've been meaning to ask you where your church is and what time the meeting starts."

She was definitely going to burn in hell if she kept lying like this.

"Don't you still have it?" Leah asked impatiently.

"Have what?"

"The pamphlet. There's a map on the back."

"No, I'm afraid it got lost."

She was so going to hell.

Mention of her church succeeded in softening the suspicion on Leah's face, although her eyes still retained some mistrust. She opened the door a little wider, leaving it open, indicating a semi-clear spot on the bed.

"Just getting some things packed," she said as she kicked the container more completely under the bed, "you can sit there."

As if there was any other place. The tiny room was already filled with the twin bed against the back wall, a nightstand to the left of the door, and a tiny, makeshift closet built on the diagonal into the back, right corner. The bed was currently covered by an open duffel bag, half-stuffed with socks, some toiletries, a brush, and what looked like Leah's bible. Leah pushed the bag aside to make room for Logan. The dingy yellow bedspread felt scratchy against the back of Logan's bare legs as she lowered herself gingerly onto it. She still had her shorts on from this morning.

Before Logan could ask Leah if she was at the festival the Sunday morning of the murder and what she may have seen, Howard called up from below.

"Leah, we're going to go get Mexican. Do you want us to bring you guys back anything—or Jared? He'll be back soon, won't he?"

Logan shook her head.

"I'm good," she said, not that Leah waited to get her order.

Leah leaned out the door toward the railing, "No, thanks. We're good. Jared's probably stuck in traffic. I'll go out and pick him up something when he gets closer. It needs to be hot."

"Okay then. Hope Jared knows how lucky he is to have you. You take good care of that boy. No cold takeout for him."

Logan thought she heard Matt grunt with disgust, followed by sounds of the two men walking out to the parking lot.

A car engine started, then silence drifted up. They were alone.

With Leah now filling the doorway, Logan suddenly felt trapped and vulnerable in the small, close room. There were no windows, only three small glass squares above the twin bed, and they didn't look like they opened. It must get awfully hot in here, she thought.

She desperately wanted to have another look at what was in that container, but after seeing what may have been one of Thomas' knives in it, she needed to get out of there and think this through.

She certainly didn't feel brave enough to confront this girl about being on the festival grounds the morning the body was discovered or why she lied about being there, let alone ask if she could go rummaging around in her personal stash of god-knew-what under the bed.

This close, she could see the young woman's thick muscles beneath her t-shirt. Although she was kind of fire-plug shaped and solid through the middle, she didn't have an ounce of fat on her. Must be from hauling around all those bags of sand for the furnace. She seemed to do all the grunt work for the glassblowers.

Leah held a wooden hanger in her right hand, tapping it absently against her left. The look on her face was not unlike Dimebox' when he looked down between his paws at one of his freshly caught mice, determining its fate.

Seeming to come to some decision, Leah tossed the hanger onto the bed. Logan tried not to flinch as it landed next to her.

Leah reached into her nightstand drawer and pulled out a pamphlet from a short stack secured with a thick rubber band.

"See," she said, flipping it over and tapping on it, "It has the directions right here—there's a map on the back."

"Oh, I must not have seen that," Logan said, "sorry to have bothered you. Do you mind if I take this one?"

She put the pamphlet in her purse and stood up to go, pulling the legs of her shorts down. The ominous feeling in the room had somewhat dispersed, so she risked asking Leah a question.

"Howard says you and Jared are going to Finland tomorrow so Jared can be in the glassblowing competition."

Leah's face brightened.

"Yes, our plane leaves early, so I won't be at church tomorrow, but if you get there by 7:30 a.m. you can meet a lot of people at the fellowship breakfast. They have donuts and coffee before the service.

"We're getting married," she added.

"Yes, I remember you and Jared are engaged."

"Yes, we're getting married sooner now, before we go to Africa. We're going on a mission there with the money Jared's going to win from the contest."

"Well, then congratulations as well as *bon voyage* is in order," Logan replied.

59

Leah said she needed to finish packing. Logan couldn't imagine what she still had left that would take much time to pack, except for whatever was under the bed. Having any conversation with this girl was awkward. This whole trip had been pointless.

"Well, I'd better be getting home, leave you to it. Tell Jared good luck with the competition," Logan said.

Leah nodded, standing in the open doorway.

When she reached the top of the stairs, Logan turned, and getting up her nerve, asked one more question that at least touched around the edges of the truth. That was, after all, the reason she came here tonight.

"You know Thomas Delgado was arrested for Elizabeth's murder, right?"

"Yeah, everyone knows that," Leah said.

"I don't believe he did it. I grew up with Thomas, he could never do anything like that."

Leah said nothing.

In for a penny, in for a pound . . .

"When you delivered those bags for me, you must have seen some of his work in the booth. Did you ever get a chance to buy any of Thomas's pieces? His obsidian knives are beautiful."

Don't push it, Logan.

Leah's eyes narrowed slightly, "No. I don't have much room here. Too expensive, anyway."

"Oh, okay."

Logan tried again from a different angle, "I was wondering about something. What do you guys do with the glass furnace at night? Do you keep it at a steady temperature, or does someone have to come in really early to heat it up? Do you help them out with that? I know you take good care of the crew."

She knew she was digging, and just hoped Leah thought it an innocent question.

"No, we lower the temperature at night, but not all the way down, and bring it back up in the morning, but it doesn't take long. If you cooled it all the way it would take hours. Why?"

Logan decided to just get it out there and ask. Leah and Jared were leaving in the morning. This was her last chance.

"I just thought maybe you had been there Sunday morning and seen something that might help the police find out who did this."

There, she'd said it.

"It was Matt's turn to open," Leah repeated, "I didn't go in at all Sunday. They called Howard and told us all to stay home after Matt found her."

Logan wasn't convinced. That jug of water didn't deliver itself.

"Well, if you think of anything, any detail, even if it seems insignificant, I'm sure the police would appreciate a call. I know Thomas would. Somebody killed that innocent girl,

Leah, and it wasn't Thomas. In fact, if you think of anything even after you leave, you can call or write to me at this address and I'll make sure the police get in touch with you."

She printed her name, cell and address on the back of an electric bill envelope she had in her purse, handing it to Leah, who folded it with one hand, pushing it down into the right side pocket of her overalls.

"I told you I wasn't there," she said, "I don't know anything about what happened to her."

"Okay," Logan said, not wanting to argue with a woman holding a potentially lethal wooden hanger. "Well, have a good trip and thanks again for the map."

As she walked down the stairs and out to her car, Logan felt drained and more confused than ever.

Whatever Leah was hiding probably had nothing to do with the murder. Logan had no authority to question her further, and doubted the police would listen to her even if she called them. Detective Andrews seemed pretty convinced he had the right man already.

She'd run it by Rick, and if the police thought it worth pursuing they could always stop Leah at the airport.

Leah had the opportunity, and possibly the means, if she had one of Thomas' knives for some reason, but no motive. As far as Logan knew, the two women spoke rarely and had little to do with one another when Elizabeth was alive. What possible reason could she have to kill her? Of course, she thought Thomas didn't know Elizabeth, either, until recently.

If she could only see what Leah hid under her bed. It was in Logan's nature to want answers, to understand fully and completely.

Right now, all she had was more questions.

60

The sun had only just set when Lola purred up the driveway, and Logan guided her into the garage. Such a luxury to hit that clicker and slide on in. Whatever had ailed her engine earlier, the drive home had worked out Lola's kinks. No pings sounded when Logan turned her off and removed the key from the ignition. She looked over at Ben's house and saw he was still up. His shadow moved back and forth across the kitchen window. The comforting, everyday sounds of running water and dishwashing noises carried across their yards as she walked to her front door. She probably missed one of his delicious BBQs.

The thought of his smile, his calm, broad face, blue eyes and big shoulders almost undid her. To have those strong arms surround her and nuzzle into that neck . . . she could feel the warmth of his skin and craved it.

She wondered if he was thinking of her.

Probably better not to invite trouble over tonight. She would invite him to Bonnie's tomorrow night for dinner, though, she decided. That was safe enough. Time to start living.

Quietly, she let herself in. She'd taken to walking around the backside of the house, to the French doors, even though the front path was shorter. There was just something about French doors that she loved. Probably the fact that no apartment they'd ever lived in had them. It was kind of a sign of home ownership. For whatever reason, they brought her joy every time she opened them.

Thirty minutes later, showered and wrapped in her robe, she decided it was too late for a wine and star-gazing session on the roof, so settled for half a glass of merlot to take up to bed and relax her to sleep. She and Ben polished off most of it a week ago, but removing the cork and sniffing the contents, she decided it was still drinkable. Her French, foreign-exchange mother would probably not have approved. She took the time to pour it through the red-wine aerator Ben had given her. It was supposed to bring out the aroma and deepen the flavors. It seemed to work, but maybe it was just the power of suggestion.

Swirling her sleep aide in her glass, she closed her eyes, breathing in the earthy aroma, then opened them to the gibbous moon outside her kitchen window. It had been almost a month since Elizabeth's murder.

So much had changed. Life itself was an ephemeral thing. Death had claimed so many already. First Jack, then, a few months later, her father was struck down by a short but vicious form of pancreatic cancer. She wondered how long she would live. Was she halfway through her life? A third? Would a truck hit her tomorrow? Logan's thoughts drifted back along her own time on earth. Like everyone else, she spent her temporal currency wantonly as if she'd never run out of the stuff.

Ben must have gone to bed—his house was dark now. In the quiet she thought of Thomas, hoping he was asleep, escaping at least for a few hours the confines of his cell and the looming trial.

SHATTERED

Lisa was on the mend. *That* worry, at least, had been lifted somewhat. Hopefully her aunt's healing ceremony would do some good, too. Who knew? Lisa believed it would. Some of the things Lisa had shared with her about native beliefs at the powwow sounded very similar to what her father said Grandma Norah tried to teach him about Appalachian herbs and planting by the signs. Did all cultures share these ancient truths and just discover them separately? So much wisdom lost. Hopefully someone somewhere was writing some of this stuff down, interviewing the old people—those who remembered how the planet and all its gifts worked.

Must be the wine, she was waxing sentimental. Polishing off the last sip, she rinsed her glass and rested it on a cotton dishtowel next to the sink. Turning off lights as she went, she took herself to bed.

In the morning, she would check in with Lisa, then Thomas to see if he'd met with his attorney yet. The best thing she could do for either of them now was to get a good night's sleep. Nothing was going to happen tonight.

61

It was all she could do not to slam the door as hard as she could, but Leah managed to control herself, shut it quietly and sit back down on the bed.

She knew!

Logan knew something, anyway. She had definitely seen her shove the box under the bed, but had she seen any of her special things? She'd done everything but come right out and ask her if she had one of Thomas' knives! She must have seen it.

Why had she left them out? She was usually so careful, tucking them safely away after touching them. No one ever saw them. But she had been careless, feeling light and giddy, knowing she and Jared were leaving in the morning, leaving all this behind.

And why was Logan asking her if she was there that morning? Had she left something behind? No, she'd been very careful cleaning up. She'd thrown the knife in the furnace. Obsidian was just natural glass. It would completely melt in high temperatures. And the bone handle would disintegrate, too.

No, there was no murder weapon to be found, nothing that could tie her to Elizabeth at all.

But if Logan told the police that she saw one of Thomas' knives here, even if it wasn't the one that had killed Elizabeth, there would be a connection. She couldn't afford to have anything delay her trip or upset Jared just before the Helsinki competition.

Sweat trickled down the small of Leah's back.

The room was stifling. She needed air. She needed to calm down. Panicking wasn't going to help. She ticked off what she knew.

First, they police weren't looking for her. They already had Thomas. The evidence against him was strong. He was being blackmailed by Elizabeth and he was there that morning. Iona saw him before Matt found the body.

Second, even if Logan saw the knife and told the police, it wasn't the murder weapon! There no longer *was* a murder weapon. Still, she didn't want her trip delayed while they figured that out.

Elizabeth was just a bad person. She deserved to die for causing all this trouble.

Leah reached for her Bible, opening it to her favorite passage, Proverbs 31, a wise mother's advice to her son, King Lemuel.

"Give not thy strength unto women, nor thy ways to that which destroyeth kings . . . "

If only Jared knew his scriptures, he may have avoided temptation and the clutches of that whore. Jared was a king, he was her king, and she would protect him.

Leah kept reading, coming to her favorite part of the scripture, the mother's description of the ideal wife.

"Who can find a virtuous woman? For her price is far above rubies. The heart of her husband doth safely trust in her, so that

he shall have no need of spoil . . . she worketh willingly with her hands . . . she bringeth her food from afar . . . she riseth while it is yet night . . . girdeth her loins with strength, and strengtheneth her arms . . . her candle goeth not out by night . . . "

Deep into the night she read, lying awake long after Jared had returned home, eaten, and gone to his room. Matt and Howard were already back and all was quiet.

Calmer now, she thought ahead to her new life with Jared.

She did not look forward to the act of giving Jared her body when they got to Finland, her only experience with sex being attacked by that horrible boy, but knew it was the right thing to do, and would bond them for life. Maybe it was different when you were married.

She wasn't worried about Jared finding out about what happened. No one knew. She'd never even confessed her sins to a pastor. Only Jesus could forgive her. The Catholics had it all wrong.

Jared need never know her failure.

Even so, the role of a woman was not an easy one. She lay on her stomach, moving her pillow aside, laying her Bible open in front of her, searching for guidance in her current situation. She was probably getting worked up for nothing.

Logan was not evil. She had been kind to her, spoken to her like she was a human being, unlike everyone else, who acted as if she weren't there, or worse, like Matt and Elizabeth, sneered at her or ordered her around.

Logan was going to church in the morning, not the police station. She made a special trip to get the map. That was a good thing. But she was friends with Thomas and would keep digging until she found a way to help him, even if it meant hurting her. Deep down, she knew that. Deep down, Leah knew Logan was Thomas' friend, not hers.

62

Not wanting anyone to hear her start up her car, she borrowed a beach cruiser Howard kept in the storage shed. She would have taken Elizabeth's bike, which was right next to it, but it was secured tightly with some indestructible, plastic-wrapped, metal chain. Besides, it was one of those racing bikes with special gears, super narrow tires and a small, hard seat. So weird. The beach cruiser was fine. She didn't need all those gears—her legs were strong.

She avoided PCH and took the back roads through town.

*****

Curled up on the bed at Logan's feet, Dimebox happily scampered around in REM-land, eyelids twitching as he pounced on a big, juicy mouse. Logan lay still, submerged in sleep and would not remember her dreams in the morning.

Neither dreamer heard the back door open, which, with everything that had been going on, Logan had failed to lock.

Leah stepped silently into the house, making her way across the living room. Pulling Thomas' knife from her backpack with her left hand, she steadied herself against the wall with her right, and carefully mounted the stairs.

She froze once, when a neighbor's dog barked, but someone came out and quieted it. Waiting for another minute before continuing, she took the last few steps quickly, anxious to get this over with and back home before anyone noticed she was gone.

Leah stopped at the top of the stairs to get her bearings.

There was only one door. She eased into the room and stood at the foot of the bed, looking down at the sleeping woman and a tabby.

Logan slept on her side, lips slightly parted, peaceful, unaware of her visitor.

Two steps farther in and she was standing right next to her.

She only wanted to silence Logan, not kill her. But she had no choice. There just wasn't any other way to guarantee she wouldn't talk.

The Lord guided her hand in righteous fury when she killed Elizabeth. She was an instrument of God. It felt good to take such evil out of the world. This was different.

She backed away softly from the bed. Stepped into the bathroom, looking for what she needed. Good. The bath towel would do. It would catch the worst of the spray. She didn't want to have to throw away another pair of overalls.

Turning the blade in her hand, she estimated the correct angle. Slowly, she leaned in, focusing on Logan's neck. Just beneath her jawbone.

She would strike quickly, mercifully. Her intent was not to be cruel. Some things just had to be done. She had to get this right. No noise.

Just then, Dimebox jumped straight up off the covers, yowling like the unholy undead. Leah raised her hand to defend herself, but the furious cat sank his claws deep into her right arm.

She only managed to nick Logan's neck before she dropped the weapon in order to fend off the cat from hell. Without thinking, she sent him flying across the room in shrieking protest. In blind panic, Leah bolted down the stairs and out the front door, her arm spurting blood.

Within seconds, a giant dog, with an even larger blonde man following on his heels, tore up the stairs and burst into Logan's room.

"Are you okay?" Ben asked, taking in the scene, "What happened? Purgatory heard something and wouldn't settle down until he dragged me over here. Who just shot out of here?"

"I'm getting all kinds of company tonight," Logan replied wanly, trying to sound composed. She sat up, legs over the side of the bed, pressing the towel Leah inadvertently dropped, on her neck, to contain the bleeding. Direct pressure. First Aid 101.

"Oh, my God!" Ben said when he saw the blood.

"I'm fine, really," Logan said, but she was shaky—either from loss of blood or realizing how close she just came to being murdered.

Dimebox, having just used up one of his nine lives, jumped up into Logan's lap, pushing against her body, purring for all he was worth. She scratched him behind his ears, comforting him in low tones while Ben called the police. She said she didn't need 911, she just wanted the police to stop Leah. She also knew she wasn't making much sense.

Leah must have killed Elizabeth, although Logan still didn't know why.

Ben washed the wound on her neck, which wasn't very deep, but scary all the same, complete with Neosporin and a large band-aid, while they waited for the police. She gladly gave up pretending she was in any kind of control and leaned against him on the couch downstairs, relaxing into his comforting side-arm grip. Usually preferring her personal space to be more ample, she was surprised she didn't mind his protective embrace.

"I'm not sure how it all fits, but I obviously rattled her cage," Logan said, explaining her conversation with Leah earlier that night, as well as everything else that had gone on that week with Lisa and Thomas. It felt good to talk it out while it was fresh in her mind.

As always, Ben was a good listener, interrupting only to ask clarifying questions or reassure. Talking with Ben was as easy as the conversations she and Thomas had shared in high school, like he was her best friend—but with sparks. Nice combination.

When they finally arrived, the officers took too much time, she thought, asking her about the attack, before sending a unit over to the compound to pick up Leah for questioning.

Now they wanted to be thorough and take their time, she thought, wishing they'd have done so before accusing Thomas so quickly. Did the police ever get it right? She didn't include Rick in her judgments. Brothers got a pass.

It sounded like that's all the police were willing to do at this point—question Leah. She'd seen her clearly. The woman had tried to slice her throat! Didn't attempted murder merit more than *questioning*?

She wanted to warn Howard. He said he was giving Leah and Jared a ride to the airport that morning. Maybe he could stall—say he had car trouble. That would buy the police a few minutes before Leah and Jared could get an Uber or a taxi.

Logan agreed with Ben, though, and the police, that involving Howard might put him in danger. No one knew what Leah would do, but they did know what she had already done. At least, tonight.

Like it or not, Logan was just going to have to wait.

63

Ben insisted on taking Logan to the ER. Surprisingly, the waiting room was empty. They took her right in, parking her in one of the curtained off treatment rooms. No one told him he couldn't, so Ben followed.

A serious looking young doctor came in with the nurse to take her vitals. It really was a slow night.

"Hello, I'm Dr. Rashmi Fitter," she said. "Let's see what we have here."

After complimenting Ben's handiwork, she asked him to wait outside while she gave Logan's wound a much deeper cleaning and whipped the wound together with a few stitches.

It hurt like hell. The cleaning hurt worse than the stitches. For those they gave her a shot of local anesthesia.

Dr. Fitter was a lot more thorough than Gentle Ben.

"You have to watch out for infection," she said. "Let me know if it becomes red or isn't healing well. Also, you'll want to follow up with your regular doctor."

Next stop, the police station, where Logan spent several hours relaying everything she'd been up to the last few weeks.

She came clean, even admitting to her illegal foray onto festival grounds the morning Elizabeth's body was found.

Given the results, Detective Andrews had a hard time getting upset with her. He seemed disinclined to do more than provide Logan with a stern lecture about leaving things in the hands of the authorities in the future. He hoped almost getting killed would be punishment enough *and* an effective deterrent.

He actually admired her persistence. He wished he had more investigators like her. To be fair, though, citizens didn't have to go by the rules. A cop's every move was scripted, caught on video, and scrutinized.

Rick laughed when he heard Andrews gave Logan a warning, knowing she would ignore his advice should the need ever arise again to put her nose where it didn't belong.

*****

They approached without lights or sirens. In the early hours of the morning, officers managed to extract a confused Jared from his room and hustle him down the stairs quietly, parking him in the back of one of the squad cars with Matt and Howard, out of danger with instructions to stay inside. With all three men removed safely from the building, the other two officers covered the exits.

Unaware of what was about to happen, Leah exited her room, duffel in hand. Seeing a policeman walk up the stairs, hand on his firearm, another walking from the right, weapon already drawn, she snarled and narrowed her eyes, but did not run.

A few minutes later, Jared watched, stunned, as they walked her, handcuffed, past him to a waiting patrol car. He barely recognized her.

SHATTERED

Back at the station, Detective Andrews and his partner had no trouble getting a full confession out of Leah. Rick heard through the grapevine that before they could even begin the questioning, she just started volunteering information. Those watching through the observation window said it was absolutely chilling to see her sitting ramrod straight, eyes shining, and hear her brag about doing God's work, how easy it had been to take Elizabeth's life, and how she cleaned up the scene and cleverly disposed of the murder weapon. She seemed particularly proud of stuffing Elizabeth's body into the annealing oven so Matt would make the gruesome discovery in the morning.

Once the whole story came out, Jared struggled to accept that the woman he had almost married was a murderer—mentally unhinged. He was also shocked by the leap she made when she thought Elizabeth's baby was his. How could she ever think that?

He had loved *Leah*, not Elizabeth! How could she not know that? How had he not seen how disturbed she was? His gentle Leah had killed another human being out of jealousy, or out of whatever was wrong with her that made her take that anger to the extreme of killing someone. He couldn't help but feel responsible for having missed the signs. Elizabeth was dead because he had been so blind.

He did not visit Leah in jail—no one did—but flew back to the Midwest to be with his family. Howard told him his place would be saved when and if he decided to return. If Howard decided to return, that is. For now, he closed down the school. Matt happily picked up the majority of the glass-blowing demos and subsequent sales for the remainder of the summer. He wasn't sentimental.

Upon Leah's arrest, Thomas was finally released—completely free to go with no restraints. No apologies, either, but at that

"

point, he didn't care. He was going home. Lisa was weak, but recovering, and able to leave the hospital. Logan talked to both of them briefly on the phone Monday afternoon.

"Of course not, don't worry about it . . . Lisa's health is more important. I'll see you when you get back. You've got the number . . . okay . . . Call if you get a chance and let me know how it goes, how she's doing. Yes, I only met her briefly, but I liked her, too. I really think this will work. I just know it will."

Lisa and Thomas had decided to go back with her Aunt to have the healing ceremony as soon as possible, then stay a while and visit relatives she hadn't seen in years. Thomas thanked her again, and Lisa asked about Ben, not missing the opportunity to tease her a little about their budding romance. Logan promised to have them over when they got back.

64

Two days later, needing to get out of the house, Logan decided to go down to Tava'e's for breakfast. She'd only been there for lunch so far. Nothing like being almost murdered to give a girl an appetite.

After her shower, she gingerly dried her stitches, dabbed on a little more antibiotic gel, and taped on a fresh, sterile gauze patch. It was healing nicely.

Letting her hair down, she fluffed her waves loosely around her neck, hoping to hide the bandage.

Not perfect, but good enough.

The comforting gurgle and hiss of espresso machines greeted her as she slipped inside Tava'e's. She spotted her favorite indulgence in the curved, glass pastry case next to the register and got in line.

Tava'e's was humming when Logan arrived, but settled into a somnolent morning after the commuters and bikers left. After paying for her cinnamon roll and a large mug of coffee, she selected a table in the back corner by the windows. If she could be Dimebox, she would have purred.

Five minutes later, licking her fingers clean of the last remnants of vanilla icing, a temporarily sated Logan settled in and sat back to people watch, sipping the last of her coffee.

Just then, the swinging doors flew open and in a burst of steam, the kitchen exhaled an enormous Polynesian woman, mopping her forehead with a white linen napkin.

This must be the infamous Tava'e.

Glancing at the pastry case as she strode by, the woman yelled back over her shoulder to the kitchen.

"Jean! No more croissants. Only rolls. Americans! They go for the frosting . . . "

"*Ca va, mon cheri,*" a deep, bass voice rang out from the kitchen. Ben said he'd never actually seen Jean, Tava'e's husband, but he was the talented creator of all the sumptuous baked goods in the case.

Logan surreptitiously wiped her fingers on the paper napkin in her lap and wished she could hide the evidence of her obviously low-class American taste in pastries.

Advancing impressively across the room, Tava'e lowered her tremendous body, enveloped in a bright, boldly patterned red and white dress, into what could only be *her* seat, at an obviously custom made, generously proportioned corner booth by the window.

Epiphany brought her boss an espresso in a gold-rimmed demi-tasse. Logan watched, fascinated, as Tava'e daintily pinched the handle between thumb and forefinger, lifting the tiny cup, delicately slurping the thick, dark mixture through sensuous, Olmec lips.

Finally, after the invisible Jean had passed fresh pastries out to Epiphany and the case was restocked, Tava'e was ready for her first true customers of the day.

SHATTERED

From a glossy wooden box, she removed a beautiful set of tall, intricately carved ebony and ivory chess pieces. The King was at least six inches high. They didn't need a board. She hadn't noticed until now, but every table in the place had a chess board painted on it already.

The setup only took a minute. They'd done this before.

The old men who had been playing outside started shuffling in.

"You ready, Tava'e?" one of them challenged.

"Ready to beat you, Charlie!" Tava'e said.

The others gathered around to watch or play a game themselves while waiting their turn. A couple of large thermoses appeared on the side counter, with a generous spread of pastries and some baguettes with ham and cheese. The homeless looking ones made their coffees thick with sugar and cream, stuffing a few packets into pockets, and one, she was sure, an entire sandwich directly under the band of his shorts.

For the next hour, Logan watched, mesmerized, as Tava'e mopped her board with them, one after the other.

The woman was amazing. If her silent mass wasn't enough to intimidate you, her supreme confidence would. She never hesitated, just firmly placed each piece down on its square, as if the end of every game were fated by Pele.

A lot of chess was played on the boardwalk; but it was clear that Tava'e's is where you went if you really wanted a good game.

Just then, Epiphany came around from behind the counter to wipe tables. Her laundry buddy sported a new assortment of piercings along with her usual heavy black eyeliner. From the safety of her sunglasses, Logan counted today's rings and studs. Lips: five, ears: four, and a new one on her right eyebrow.

That must have hurt.

Logan liked the girl's quiet competence. She took care of every customer quickly and politely, without fawning. In fact, without speaking, much of the time. You had to respect people who didn't try too hard.

Logan was so engrossed in inventorying Epiphany's facial hardware, she didn't notice when Ben came in, leaving the faithful Purgatory sleeping in the shade under a table outside.

"I got your message you'd be down here," he said, "How's the neck?"

"Oh, hi, Ben. It's good. Thanks for taking me Sunday."

"No trouble."

"I still can't believe it. It all seems so surreal," said Logan.

"Yeah, but it's over," Ben said.

"Rick said Leah will probably plead insanity."

"Not much of a stretch there. Did Thomas and Lisa make it out okay?" he asked.

"Yes, they should be landing right about now," Logan said.

Epiphany materialized at their table.

"What can I get you?" she asked.

Logan wanted another cinnamon roll, but resisted, settling instead for a refill on her coffee. She had yet to differentiate between Zimbabwe and Organic Colombian. Whatever they had on tap was what she ordered. Today's roast was Ethiopian. Ben matched her coffee selection, but surprisingly, had only a small brioche and waved off offers of cream or sugar.

"Been putting on a little too much padding," he said ruefully, rubbing his stomach.

Ben did have some extra insulation; but with the Norwegian trifecta of perfect white teeth, square jaw and an open, honest face, Logan didn't mind. Add the smiling blue eyes, and you'd trust him with your first-born. She again wondered why he hadn't been snapped up.

Morning traffic was flowing more than ebbing by the time Tava'e, who had just finished beating another opponent, spotted Ben. She made her way over to their table, engulfed him in a huge hug, and pressed her massive cheek against his.

"*Talofa*! Where have you been? Eat! Eat! You are too skinny, my friend!"

Ben returned the hug and assured her he was fine, just had been busy. He sat down and Tava'e stepped back, turning her attention to Logan.

"Don't think you're getting away without another cinnamon roll, little one," she said.

"The two of you could blow away with a good wind", she muttered, waving to Epiphany, who was already heading over to the table with said rolls, anticipating her boss' request.

Logan had no choice but to accept the aromatic offering.

What could she do? She couldn't be rude . . .

After setting down the rolls, Epiphany continued to the front door, grabbing a helmet and her leather jacket from the coat rack as she exited. Not to anyone's surprise, she mounted a motorcycle. Silver lip rings glinting in the sun, she revved the engine, turned her handlebars south, and roared down PCH.

"Okay! Down to business. How do you like your house?" Tava'e asked.

Until now, Logan had viewed Tava'e as something like one of those imposing Easter Island monoliths, holding court, but she seemed less intimidating now that she had spoken.

"I wish I could have met the previous owner. Meg, right? She sounds like a very interesting person," Logan added, really meaning it.

"Those relatives of hers come poking around?" Tava'e sniffed with disapproval.

"Yes" Logan smiled at the thought of the awful couple, "but they didn't stay long".

"They hightailed it back to Indiana once they got their money," said Ben. "With a little shove from this one, I have a feeling," he jerked a thumb in Logan's direction.

"And a pox on them! Meg did not belong to them. She belonged with us!" Tava'e declared, adamantly.

Logan felt as if by buying the house, she had inherited a neighborhood family, which felt comforting and terrifying at the same time. What if she didn't measure up?

Tava'e was still talking.

". . . Meg never learned to play chess. You will not make that same mistake!"

What?

Had she missed something? When had she promised to learn to play chess?

"We will start today!" Tava'e began making her way back to her booth, indicating with a regal wave of her hand that Logan was to follow.

Ben stood and stretched. "Well, I guess I'm leaving you to a chess lesson. Purgatory and I have some business to attend to, so we're going to head back. Catch you later."

Not feeling she had much of a choice, Logan docilely followed Tava'e and took her place on the opposite side of the table.

"It's very easy," Tava'e stated, pinning Logan with large, ebony eyes, daring her to contradict.

Tava'e showed her how the pieces were set up.

"White square on the right. Queen on her own color."

Then she explained the game, "Just a king, a queen, and an army trying to protect the King. It is the man needs protecting, not the woman," she said, with a sidelong glance at the kitchen.

"Sixty-four squares. Don't worry about naming them now-- A1, H5 . . . I do not bother with that. For today, we will just learn how the pieces move."

For the next thirty minutes, Logan learned that the King, although the entire focus of the game, could only move one square at a time, while the Queen could move as many spaces as she wanted in any direction. She learned that pawns were only worth one point, but should not be given away need- lessly. Every piece, even the seemingly insignificant, was worth something.

The only thing she wound up remembering on her walk home an hour later, beyond the king's one step and the bish- op's sweeping, long-range attacks, was that the knight was cool. He was sneaky, moving in a zigzag, L-shape and was the only piece who could jump.

They tried one game and she hadn't yet figured out why the rook was worth five points and the horse, "Knight," Tava'e corrected, was worth only three points. Her rooks had stayed trapped in their corners.

Apparently hers were cowards, as Tava'e's were front and center within a few moves, after she did something called castling, which she said protected her king and should be done as soon as possible. Castling reminded Logan of trying to watch football. Everyone was in neat rows, there was some scrambling, and then it was over and the ball had somehow moved.

It had been surprisingly fun. There'd been a chess club at school, of course, but no one was clamoring to join. All she remembered about the five members of her high school chess club was that they must have had more than a hundred-and- fifty zits between them. She was ashamed to realize how shallow she'd been in high school. She'd never been a mean girl, but she hadn't reached out to anyone, either. She had Thomas and Bonnie, then Jack. They were all pretty self-centered.

When she felt a stabbing pain in her left toe, Logan knew her sitting time was up. Ever since the accident her sciatic nerve had given her trouble if she stayed in one position too long. She quickly leaned to the right. Instantly the worst of the pain let up, but she knew it would only get worse if she ignored it and didn't get up and get moving.

She checked her watch. It was only 10:00 a.m. If she was going to get a jump on Monday's job boards, she'd better get a move-on. Bonnie and Mike got back from their trip last night. At least she had dinner at their place to look forward to.

65

She spent the best part of the last hour selecting and rejecting various combinations of her spartan wardrobe. Next time Bonnie wanted to drag her to the mall, she'd have to give in.

Two minutes before Ben got there, she settled on jeans and the blue silk sweater she'd worn the night he came over for dinner. She couldn't help visualizing him slipping it off her shoulders. He had the best hands: warm and rough—perfect, like the rest of him.

She heard a knock on the door.

Was it 6:30 p.m. already?

She reapplied her lip-gloss, pushed at her hair in the mirror, going for the wholesome, sexy look, and hurried downstairs. Nervously, she scratched her nose before opening the door.

Ben looked her over and smiled, "You look great!"

He handed her a pot of bright yellow flowers, "These keep longer than the cut ones. I'll put them in for you tomorrow, if you want. Make you remember our first official date."

She set them down by the door, then picked up the gift for Bonnie she'd left there so she wouldn't forget it. She shivered a little when she remembered the day Leah had brought the bags to her at Thomas & Lisa's booth. That was probably the day she had stolen Thomas' knives.

Ben looked good.

A Tommy Bahama shirt in creamy neutrals set off his china blue eyes and, of course, the blonde hair. Simple watch. Nice. Soft blue jeans. Leather topsiders. No socks. Even the tops of his feet were sexy.

As they walked to the car, she noticed her head would fit right into the curve of his shoulder if they were lying down. She allowed her mind to linger on that thought.

He drove. She'd promised him a spin in Lola, although normally she didn't let anyone drive her car. Lola didn't seem to mind. In fact, she responded to Ben's touch with pleasure, purring louder than usual. She brought them smoothly to Bonnie's door in record time.

Ben carried a 2005 Cabernet/Syrah and Logan's birthday gift for Bonnie, the yellow bowl she bought for her at the festival, up to the door.

A very tan and relaxed-looking Bonnie, her blonde curls restrained by a bright, red headband, answered and gave Logan and then Ben, a big hug, accepting her gifts. She was wearing a flowing white cotton skirt brightly embroidered with tropical birds and flowers. Very Bonnie!

After ushering Ben in, she gave Logan an enthusiastic double thumbs-up and a silent, "Wow!" of approval.

Mike didn't tan, so his nose was on its third or fourth layer of peeling from what they learned were several deep-sea fishing trips.

"You shoulda seen the bluefin, Ben! Great charter, too. We'll get them again next time. You should come with us. We're going back next year, if we can. Do you like to fish?"

Ben did. He and Mike swapped stories 'til dinner was ready.

SHATTERED

As always at Bonnie and Mike's, dinner was delicious and the noise, deafening. After the huge meal, the kids went into the den to play video games, while the adults settled in the living room for single shots of an intense blackberry after-dinner liqueur they'd discovered on their previous vacation to Oregon. From Puerto Vallarta, Bonnie had brought Logan back a silver bracelet and some hot sauce she swore would rival even the Fire Fries sauce at Phoenix Burgers.

Bonnie loved the glass bowl, taking it into the kitchen, filling it with fruit immediately. She gave it pride of place in the center of the big dining room table, which had been cleared by two of her children. She had them well trained. It was their night to do the dishes. They were quick about it and had already joined their siblings in the den to watch TV.

"Okay, let's get to the important stuff—my news!" Bonnie herded them back into the living room and sat them on the couch.

In all the excitement of the last few days, Logan had completely forgotten about the news Bonnie said she had to share.

"First, what are you doing next Tuesday, Logan?" Bonnie's brown eyes glowed with mischief. She could hardly contain herself.

"Tuesday? Uh . . ."

"Because you might want to leave that night open, and plan on attending the school board meeting," her friend-turned-Cheshire-cat said.

"Just tell her," Mike said.

"Okay, okay. We got in around noon, and after we checked in, I went down to get a massage. You need to get your massage early, before you get sunburned. Anyway, after my massage, I was all relaxed, sitting there getting a mani-pedi, and guess who sat down in the chair next to me?"

Not waiting for an answer, she continued, "Charles Greuger's wife!"

"Who's Charles Greuger?" Logan asked, confused.

"Charles Greuger is only one of the most influential members of the school board, *and* is good friends with the superintendent."

Still not seeing how this applied to her, Logan waited for her friend to finish, knowing it would do no good to rush her.

"Well, I told her all about you, about what you brought to your job, your music, how you got along so well with the kids, and about what happened to you . . . "

"You didn't . . . "

"I did, but it's okay. By the time our toes were dry, she said not to worry, she had an idea."

It turns out they're big music fans, and no fans at all of Metterson. Their son went to his school. She said he's at Stanford in spite of him. She didn't know Sheila, but said she's seen her kind before. I figured what the hell? I'm there, she's there. Couldn't hurt!"

Logan grimaced.

"Well, it was obvious *you* weren't going to do anything," Bonnie said in her own defense.

"I know your heart was in the right place, but I don't want someone else to fix my problems," Logan said. It's not like her summer hadn't been busy, but Bonnie was right, She had to do something soon, or her teaching career would end before it started.

After filling them in on Lisa's upcoming healing ceremony, they gossiped about Rick's interest in the new dispatcher. The conversation ended with mango salsa recipes. Ben wanted to try one out this weekend.

After thanking her friends for dinner, and Bonnie's well-intentioned, if impulsive, interference in her work problems, she and Ben walked out to the car. Bonnie's eyebrows raised when Ben got behind the wheel.

Logan promised to call Grueger in the morning. She had to admit, she was curious.

66

What Charles Grueger had in mind was beyond anything Logan could have hoped for. With the adoption of the new Common Core standards, subjects previously taught in isolation under *No Child Left Behind* were now to be integrated, with non-tested and often under-valued subjects such as Music, Drama, PE, and the Visual Arts. The standards were, he said, still too broad, but Common Core was a step in the right direction.

"It will be a mess for a few years, but at least it'll keep the testing vultures off our backs for a while," he added with surprising candor, "they'll have a devil of a time trying to nail us to the wall with test scores until they work out the kinks with the new state-wide assessments."

Logan's eyes started to glaze over when he started talking about testing, but he spoke with a frankness Logan had not yet heard from anyone in education besides Bonnie. It was good to know common sense prevailed somewhere. Her excitement grew as he outlined what he had in mind, and how she fit in.

"Gail and I—have you met Gail? You'll be working for her directly. Very good woman. We've hammered out an initial plan, an outline, really. We need an expert to fill in the gaps, to design a workable program—someone who knows music and math, and comes from outside the school system. Creative, entrepreneurial. A business exec with an artsy side. Preferably a musician."

He took a breath.

"Bonnie tells my wife you play."

Seeing the surprise on her face, he laughed. "Seriously, we've checked your education and spoken with several parents of students in your class at the middle school. All excellent. And you should know that several parents went to bat for you. And don't worry about your credential, this program will fit nicely into the university's intern credential program.

If you're interested, I'd like to show you what we have so far and hear your ideas. Mrs. Houser's already a fan, so we've got a decent budget to work with. She's providing the seed money to get it off the ground, and the district's willing to allocate a percentage of the Common Core budget if this first year is successful.

For the next few hours, stopping only for a quick box lunch his assistant ordered in, they poured over plans and brainstormed.

It was only after she returned home, happy and exhausted, but bursting at the seams to share her news with Bonnie and Ben, she realized he'd made no mention of Metterson's letter.

She wouldn't find out until next week, but it was worth the wait. At the end of the board meeting, after her appointment as director of the new program was announced, several inter-district principal transfers were mentioned, including one for a Philip Metterson, who would now head the James Polk Continuation School, located at the edge of the district, an extra hour's drive from his home.

SHATTERED

After calling Bonnie with the good news, she went over to Ben's to give him a complete update. He wanted to treat her to dinner, but after a glass of wine and some excellent cheese and crackers she begged off until the next night, needing some rooftop time to process everything.

"You're off the hook until tomorrow, McKenna," he said playfully, pulling her in for a kiss, which warmed her to her very toes.

"I'll pick you up at 6:00 p.m. Dress up," he called as she walked back to her place, "We'll go someplace special."

She loved that he understood her need to be alone sometimes. She didn't know if she could have articulated her feelings if he'd asked.

*****

It was a great luxury not to be rushed. Jack had given her the full-court press until she agreed to marry him, breathless and flattered at his ardent pursuit. He had probably done the same with the former owner of the pink shoebox. She shook her head at her youthful naïveté.

Yesterday, she'd taken the box out of the closet and rifled through it. The woman had printed out each email, copied every note, card, ticket stub, and cocktail napkin, arranging them all chronologically, proving Jack's relationship with her had lasted at least a year. Probably to prove to her that they were serious, that Jack loved her. Logan was just glad she, not Amy, had discovered the box on their doorstep the morning of the funeral.

Part of her wanted to angrily confront the woman, find out the exact details. How many other pink-shoebox-owners had there been? Was she lacking somehow that Jack needed to look elsewhere? Had he ever really loved her? But in the end, it was surprisingly easy to throw the box, its contents, and any lingering questions, off the rocks at the end of Main Beach.

If Jack had lived, she would have confronted *him*, not the woman. They may have worked things out and grown up together, but probably not. She didn't know if she was the forgiving type. It didn't matter now. What mattered was the life she had now. The one she fully intended to live.

Later, when the sun finished tracing its path across the sky, Logan sat in the soft darkness, comfortable in her chair, Dimebox curled against her leg, completely as happy as animals and their humans get. Dimebox hadn't strayed far since Leah's attack that night.

Ben sent her home with the rest of the bottle of Pinot Noir, which she was now enjoying, savoring each mouthful as her French mother had taught her, slowly, taking great pleasure in simple things.

A few powerful stars managed to poke through the coastal clouds still obscuring the constellations. She could make out the Big Dipper, or was that Orion's belt? Someday she'd have to learn those.

School was only two months away. She started her new job Monday. So much to do, but she looked forward to the new challenge. It was the perfect balance of creative freedom, meaningful work, and a steady paycheck. Now she could pay for that cool rocking chair!

Ned and Sally had agreed to help. The kids were going to love them, she knew. She already had several of last year's students in mind as project leaders.

Ben was carving out some time from his landscaping jobs and, with a friend of his, was going to build her a sound studio. The district was thrilled not to have to find her any office space, she'd work above the studio. She hadn't broken it to Lola yet that she was losing her garage again, but the prospect of working from home, traveling as needed to the three schools who volunteered for the pilot program, was a perfect setup for her. Hopefully, Lola would understand.

No more Metterson, and no more *Sheila*! There would be others like them along the way, she was sure, but she felt more prepared to deal with them now.

She took another sip of the excellent wine. Amy was bringing Liam home for Thanksgiving, and the Pacific Ocean was as awe-inspiring as ever. It spread its silvery skirts before her, glittering on the navy sea, under a wide-open sky. Plenty of room to breathe.

Her home was coming along and Tava'e had praised her opening moves yesterday, said she had a much better command of the board.

Tilting her head back, she drank in the tangy, salty air, and closed her eyes. In the stillness, she listened to the mesmerizing waves, her thoughts drifting lazily on the rhythmic sounds.

Sometime later, Dimebox jumped down and, after a good cat stretch, headed down the stairs to begin his nightly rounds. Logan started gathering her things, thinking about her new life. She had a lot to look forward to, including dinner tomorrow night with Ben.

The delighted shiver that ran up her spine had little to do with the cold.

ACKNOWLEDGMENTS

The challenge of writing a novel isn't coming up with ideas. Most writers walk around with plots and characters in their heads 24/7. We're just wired that way. You never know when or where inspiration will strike.

Iona Slatterly, for example, one of my favorite characters, was inspired by a woman I met while doing jury duty. I have no idea what her real job was, but it was fun recreating the platinum beehive and spray-on pink jeans in the pages of *Shattered*.

No, the real challenge in writing a novel is keeping all the plot lines from tangling, making sure you don't lead your reader down a dead-end road, or call the restaurant Juan's in one chapter and Jose's in the next. All of which I have done.

You can't write a book alone, so I'd like to thank the many talented and hard working people who helped me in the writing, polishing, design, and publishing of this new version of *Shattered*.

Just a word here for readers who enjoyed the story the first time around. The story remains the same, I've just moved the action forward a few chapters and streamlined the interior to make for smoother reading. I have also kept all your favorite characters, including Iona!

Jennifer Sears Glass Art Studio in Lincoln City, OR allowed me to experience glassblowing first hand. Pardon the pun, but Michelle and I had a blast! I'd also like to thank John Barber, veteran Laguna Beach, CA glassblower who patiently explained the process, temperatures, and materials that go into the art. My thanks also to all of the glassblowers at the Sawdust Festival and in Lincoln City, who took the time to answer my many questions. Any remaining errors in the book are all mine.

Terry Baxter of WesternArtifacts.com shored up my Archaeology 101 knowledge of obsidian knives, and many others humored me by answering emails and spending time with me on the phone explaining arcane details such as how much a jingle dress weighs. And thanks to family, friends, and my wonderful Beta Readers, who gave me great feedback before sending it on its way to the awesome Sandra McClintock for editing, and creative powerhouse Kim Peticolas for the perfect cover and clean interior design.

My husband, John, wins the perfect husband award for understanding when the Logan light is on. He gives me the gift of time and quiet within which to write. I couldn't do it without him. The hot coffee and shoulder rubs are appreciated, too.

And last but not least, I'd like to thank you, the reader, for purchasing and reading my books, allowing me to continue doing what I love.

ABOUT THE AUTHOR

A self-admitted book addict, Valerie Davisson was the kid with the flashlight under her pillow, reading long after lights out. After a life of travel, she now lives on the Oregon coast with her husband, John, and their new puppy, Finn. When not working on her latest book, she's probably in the kitchen, cooking up a storm for family and friends.

Enjoyed the Book?

If you enjoyed this book, please consider leaving a review on Amazon or Goodreads. And be sure to check out the rest of the Logan McKenna series.

Forest Park (Book 2)

Devil's Claw (Book 3)

Vanishing Day (Book 4)

Safe Harbor (Book 5)

Lies That Bind (Book 6)

Whisper Creek (Book 7)

In Plain Sight (Book 8)

Want to know more about Valerie Davisson or her next book? Make sure to visit www.valeriedavisson.com and sign up for her newsletter.

The Logan McKenna Series

The Logan McKenna Series

The Logan McKenna Prequels